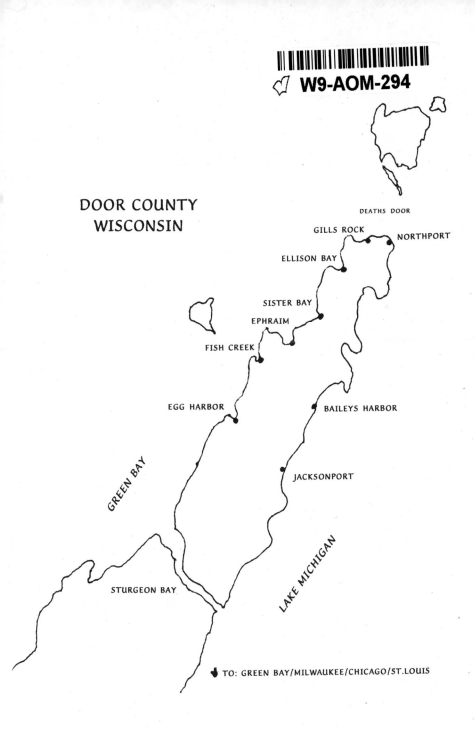

W9-AOM-294

DOOR COUNTY
WISCONSIN

DEATHS DOOR

GILLS ROCK

NORTHPORT

ELLISON BAY

SISTER BAY

EPHRAIM

FISH CREEK

EGG HARBOR

BAILEYS HARBOR

GREEN BAY

JACKSONPORT

LAKE MICHIGAN

STURGEON BAY

TO: GREEN BAY/MILWAUKEE/CHICAGO/ST.LOUIS

Kathleen Arnold, Ann Kurz Chambers
Ilse Dietsche, Justin Isherwood, DyAnne Korda
Jackie Langetieg, Mary "Casey" Martin
Edith Nash, Steve Raap, Mariann Ritzer
Barbara Fitz Vroman, Gloria Zager,
and poet, Dorianne Laux

PERMISSIONS:
DORIANNE LAUX: "This Close" copyright 1994, by Dorianne Laux.
Reprinted from WHAT WE CARRY with the permission of
BOA Editions, Ltd., 260 East Ave., Rochester, NY 14604.
and
JEANNE LARSON HYDE, author of HAZEL'S KITCHEN TABLE, copyright 1997
Palmer Publications, 318 North Main St., Amherst, WI 54406.

CONCEIVED/DESIGNED/EDITED BY
Mary "Casey" Martin
EDITORIAL ASSISTANT
DyAnne Korda
COVER ARTIST
Holly Hebel

Coming Home to Door
Vignettes & Recipes
Celebrating the 100th Anniversary of the Door County Literary Guild/
Mary "Casey" Martin
Fiction. / Cookbook.

Library of Congress Catalog Card Number: 98-94136

FIRST EDITION
ISBN 1-891609-05-X

Designed, Marketed & Published
by

HOME BREW PRESS
a division of The Martin Agency
2540 Abby Lane - P.O. Box 185
Wisconsin Rapids, WI 54495-0185
Ph/FAX: 715.421.2429
FAX ORDERS: 800.250.2986
VOICEMAIL/PAGER: 888.492.4531

ACKNOWLEDGEMENTS

The cover art was created by Holly Hebel, Egg Harbor. The work is titled, "Thursday Afternoon" and was purchased by Sue and Louie Andrew, who also gave their permission for use of the artwork on the cover. This primitive blue house represents the blue skies and waters surrounding "the Door." A colorful clothesline and home represent the women of the fictional guild. Cedar trees are prevalent throughout the peninsula and help frame the rustic home. John Maniaci photographed the art for reproduction.

Special thanks to Dorianne Laux, the poet, for the use of her poem, "This Close", from her book *What We Carry* which appears in the chapter titled, "May Interlude" written by Mariann Ritzer.

A number of people were kind enough to offer their time to read the manuscript before it went to press. Besides the writers themselves, they are: Barbara & Bill Cammack, Chuck & Elaine Davis, Bridget Doyle, Kathleen Finnerty, Helen J. Lautenbach, Barbara Kramer, Linda Raap, Janet Suzda, V.V., Mary Lou Wangen and Christie Weber.

One of the contributors, DyAnne Korda, also acted as assistant editor and provided me with many words of encouragement throughout the process of developing my idea into this collaborative work.

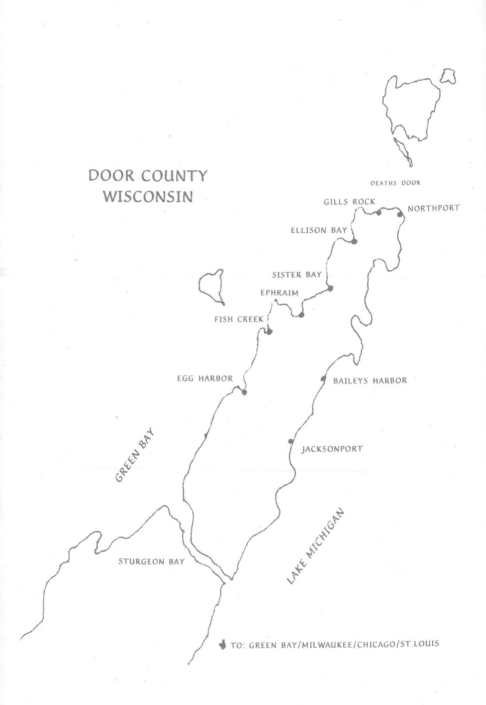

DOOR COUNTY
WISCONSIN

DEATHS DOOR

GILLS ROCK

NORTHPORT

ELLISON BAY

SISTER BAY

EPHRAIM

FISH CREEK

EGG HARBOR

BAILEYS HARBOR

GREEN BAY

JACKSONPORT

LAKE MICHIGAN

STURGEON BAY

TO: GREEN BAY/MILWAUKEE/CHICAGO/ST.LOUIS

VIGNETTES & RECIPES

*Celebrating the 100th Anniversary of
The Door County Literary Guild*

Coming Home to Door

WORKS OF FICTION

by

Kathleen Arnold   Ann Kurz Chambers   Ilse Dietsche
Justin Isherwood   DyAnne Korda   Jackie Langetieg
Mary "Casey" Martin   Edith Nash   Steve Raap
Mariann Ritzer   Barbara Fitz Vroman   Gloria Zager
and poet, Dorianne Laux

CONCEPT BY MARY "CASEY" MARTIN

HOME BREW PRESS

bluestocking
n: a woman with intellectual interests

An upper-crust
18th-century ladies' literary group,
was orginally called the"bluestocking society"
when a poor, yet distinquished, male guest speaker
was made welcome
even though he only wore blue worsted stockings
instead of the formal black silk.
It was all he could afford.
The term became a symbol of
intellectualism over materialism.
It was a derisive label that was eventually
adopted by the members themselves.

INTRODUCTION

by
Mary "Casey" Martin

There was never any intention of resemblence to any living or deceased persons. While the towns and names of businesses may in some cases be real, anything that happens in a community or business is fictional.

This book is a collaboration with twelve writers for a fictional concept created by me, the editor. The idea was going to be used for my first novel and it needed twelve main characters. Then it hit me. *What better way to get twelve different characters, than have twelve different writers create them.*

I wrote a list of main ingredients, along with the concept and solicited the writers. Each writer was given the core ingredients, but also creative license to reveal the personality of their invented club member.

MAIN INGREDIENTS: 1. Membership in the same fictional book club, The Door County Literary Guild. 2. Act as hostess for a monthly meeting. 3. Introduce the reader to their member's book selection and author for their monthly meeting. 4. Describe a Door County location where the meeting would be held and/or the personality of the guild member through journal entries, letters, reminiscence, etc. 5. Optional: provide a recipe that would be served to the guild members.

LOCATION: Being born and raised on the Door County peninsula, I knew it to be a popular U.S. tourist destination. Located on Wisconsin's East Coast, the Door peninsula has 250 miles of shoreline.

Growing up on "the Door" and working at my family's supperclub, I served Bob Hope dinner and met the actor, Jack Carson. *June Allison was shopping in Ephraim. Charlton Heston is at Gordon Lodge.* Sitings of the rich and famous always ran rampant throughout "the County." But, I've always believed it is the local characters that make a place interesting.

I requested that the writers invent residents or transplants who live on the peninsula in the year 1998. Each writer wrote their chapter independent of the others, not seeing the entire book until months later. They had one opportunity for their own edit of their chapter. The pieces stand on their own and retain each writer's voice, but are connected through one concept-- their members belong to the same club.

CONCEPT: The fictional Door County Literary Guild is celebrating its 100th Anniversary in 1999. A Green Bay television reporter comes to interview the book club president during the day of the anniversary dinner. The other members of the guild are revealed month by month (from February through December 1998). The last chapter will bring the reader back to the anniversary month in the year 1999. Twelve, very different, women come together through their love of books and their experiences and become lifelong friends.

Get ready for an interesting, fun read! I hope you enjoy meeting the members of the oldest club in Door County and I encourage you to try the recipes at the back of the book the next time you have to host a meeting or an event for your club or organization.

Within these pages are references to numerous titles and authors. The Guild's Reading List is provided at the back of the book, after the recipes. So, if you don't know what to read next, read on.

MARY "CASEY" MARTIN
Publisher/Writer

P.S. The four pages that follow include an alphabetical listing of the contributing writers and a brief real life bio about each of them and background information about the cover artist.

P.P.S. "Chapter by Chapter" on page xvii will introduce you to the members of The Guild and the writers who created them.

WRITERS' BIOGRAPHIES
An Alphabetical Listing of the Contributing Writers

KATHLEEN ARNOLD was born and raised in Wisconsin Rapids, WI. She has one daughter. Kathleen holds a management position in the banking industry. Her creative outlets are literature, music and gardening.

ANN KURZ CHAMBERS is an artist and writer who lives in Colorado at her moutain top cabin and at a home in Grand Junction. She continues to find peace and solace in her mountain home where she paints rock walls and Plains Indian designs on elk and deer skins.

ILSE DIETSCHE is an international traveler and photographer. Her photographs have been published in *A Portrait of Everyday Life in Wisconsin* and her poetry, as well as photos, appeared in *the poetry of cold - a collection of writings about winter, wolves & love*. Ilse, originally from Emmendingen, Germany, now lives in Wisconsin Rapids, WI.

JUSTIN ISHERWOOD is a fifth generation farmer and the author of numerous titles including, *The Book of Plough-Essays on Rural Life*. His articles and essays have appeared in *Reader's Digest* and *Audubon Magazine*. A new book, *Wisconsin Seasons*, will include one of his stories. He's been a guest on National Public Radio's *Whad' Ya Know? with Michael Feldman*, Wisconsin Public Radio and Wisconsin Public Television. He writes a column for the *Stevens Point Journal* and is a contributor to *Wisconsin River Valley Journal*. Justin lives with his wife, Lynn, in Plover, WI. They have two grown children.

DYANNE KORDA is a poet, writing tutor, and artist. She has been published in magazines such as *Wise Woman's Garden, Hodge Podge Poetry*, and *Wisconsin Poets' Calendar*. She has five collections of poetry including, *Finding the Lost Woman* (Cross+Roads Press). Korda lives with her husband, Scott, and their cats in Stevens Point, WI.

JACKIE LANGETIEG lives in Madison, WI. where she writes poetry and fiction. She has two grown sons. She has published fiction in *Rosebud, Peninsula Review, Tasty Morsels* and *Detours II* and poetry in *Midland Review, 100 Words* and Wisconsin Fellowship of Poets calendar.

MARY "CASEY" MARTIN is a photographer, poet, writer and publisher of Home Brew Press and owner of The Martin Agency--a public relations, design and talent agency. She has represented mostly Wisconsin talent, including the late Dr. Frances Hamerstrom. Her first collaborative effort, *the poetry of cold - a collection of writings about winter, wolves & love*, received an award, Certificate of Merit for Outstanding Accomplishment in the Writer's Digest 1997 National Self-Publishing Competition. A sequel titled, *muddy water - a book about fishing, friendships & wildflowers* is planned. Born and raised on the Door peninsula, she divides her time between Egg Harbor and Wisconsin Rapids, WI.

EDITH NASH is a poet and writer. She has studied writing under Norbert Blei at The Clearing in Ellison Bay, WI. Edith coordinates a writer's group in Wisconsin Rapids, WI. She lived in the nation's capital during the Truman and Kennedy administrations. As well as her self-published chapbooks, her work has appeared in numerous issues of *Wisconsin River Valley Journal* and the *Wisconsin Poets' Calendar.*

STEVE RAAP is a professional advertising writer. He lives with his wife, Linda, in Nekoosa, WI. His first career was in television production. Steve has since worked in various corporate marketing and advertising agency positions and is currently working on his first novel.

MARIANN RITZER teaches and writes in Hartland at Waukesha County Technical College and in Door County at The Clearing. She has published two chapbooks of poetry, *An Evening on Mildred Street* (Cross+Roads Press), and *How To Fall Out of Love* (Wolfsong Publications) which ranked in the top ten in Pippistrelle Best of Small Press Awards, as did her chapbook of fiction, *Once I Loved Him Madly* (Cross+Roads Press). Her short story, "Objects Appear Closer Than They Are," won honorable mention in the Cardinal Stritch Wordspring Writing Contest in 1998.

BARBARA FITZ VROMAN is the author of *Linger Not at Chebar*, *Sons of Thunder*, and *Tomorrow is a River* (co-authored by Peggy Hanson Dopp). Barbara also writes short stories and articles. She is twice recipient of the Milwaukee Journal Leslie Cross Award for best novel of a Wisconsin writer in the year of publication. Twice Barbara also received the Wisconsin Regional Writers' Jade Ring Award. She lives in Hancock, WI.

GLORIA ZAGER is a world traveler, photographer and writer. Retired from Georgia Pacific in 1997, she continues her ornithological studies around the world with Earth Watch. She lives with her husband and son in Vesper, WI.

ABOUT THE COVER ARTIST:

HOLLY HEBEL is by trade a woodworker, a storyteller, a master fishboiler, a student of art and social sciences, and a history buff. She is an outdoor enthusiast and recreational therapist. Holly has grown up surrounded by the fields of Wisconsin and the waters of Lake Michigan. Her works incorporate the past and present, interpreting objects of yesterday with contemporary use of color. Door County has been her home for over ten years. She lives in Egg Harbor, WI.

TABLE OF CONTENTS

Table of Contents

CHAPTER BY CHAPTER

xvii

KATHERINE "KATE" MURPHY

The January Interview
by
Mary "Casey" Martin

Kate Murphy, a freelance writer, lives in the house she inherited from her grandmother. The large, white colonial stands prominently overlooking the village of Egg Harbor. Kate loves the house, but the maintenance of it is wearing a thin red line on her savings account. With its wide center staircase and two great rooms in each wing, entertaining is a joy. On the left side of the staircase are the double doors leading into the study where tonight she will host the anniversary dinner for the Door County Literary Guild.

Melanie Richards, a Green Bay television reporter, was running an hour late. The tall, slender blonde was assigned the interview highlighting the peninsula's oldest "bookclub."

Steel-eyed Kate Murphy, short in stature and sometimes in attitude, hated waiting for anything or anyone--even if it was for a good cause. *I hate this. If I start something new, she will show up for sure. Maybe I could review the final draft of that new piece*

1

for the <u>Door County Magazine</u>? *No, I don't want to be interrupted on that one. I only have a few days to complete it--make the deadline--so I get paid. And I need that check. I have to test that new recipe, the one for <u>Le Bon Fomme,</u> but actually I'm looking forward to that. I should have fixed the chowder for lunch today and killed two birds . . . Chimes ringing . . . Saved by my "Door" bell. What does Inge always say; "Ring my weathered bell." That's exactly how I feel today. Now I have to do this TV interview. There's so much to do before I leave.*

Kate puts down her copy of *And Ladies of the Club* and extends her hand to the Green Bay television reporter, "Hello. Welcome to Murphy's Xanadue."

"Hi, I'm Melanie Richards, Channel 5 News." Then Melanie apologized, "My ace camera crew is late due to another accident we had to cover. It's so hard to cover those sad stories. Saying good-bye to loved ones is difficult, especially when it's an unexpected death. I'm glad you and I will be talking about something more positive today. So . . ."

Kate interrupted, "I've been reviewing some of the minutes from the Guild, but after 100 years it is difficult to condense the information for a one-minute blurb on the local news. If anyone can do it, Melanie, you can." She added, "I enjoy your style of reporting, and really like the profiles of some of the area's local characters. After we get through with this interview, you'll have even more personalities you can make famous."

Melanie wanted to get some of the back story on the Guild. She queried Kate, "What is the actual anniversary date of Door County's oldest book club?"

"The Guild was formed on January 29, 1899. So this

2

year is the commemorative 100th Birthday Bash. Oh man, wouldn't the founding members shudder at that use of the English language !" Kate continued, "The Door County Literary Guild was originally an invitation-only organization. Members were brought to an afternoon tea. If they survived the formalities, they were invited for a return visit which included their induction ceremony. If you weren't on the A list, you didn't have a prayer of getting in. Very haughty attitudes prevailed for the first 30 years. The Depression years tended to temper most of the members. By the end of it, they were just thankful to keep the meetings going. The minutes of the meetings do reveal a lot. Today it's more informal. The meetings are still held at members' homes and on rare occasions we dine out. We are blessed in this tourist area with so many fine dining places . . . Casey's? Common House? English Inn? Trio? Inn at Kristofer's? Sometimes we decide to avoid the whole ordeal and do a potluck."

"Is that part of the regular schedule? Do you meet monthly or every other month?" Melanie was trying to get the basics down on paper, before any taping began.

"We try for monthly. Some of the members have their own businesses, and some actually commute, so it's difficult for everyone to show up every month. Most businesses are tied into the tourist industry. It's not like the old days when Labor Day would provide the parade of cars heading South. We would all sit inside the C&C Club and celebrate the passing of another summer. Now the county-wide Spring Daffodil's Season blends into Baileys Harbor's Fourth of July Parade, followed by Egg Harbor's Pumpkin Patch and the Fall Festival in Sister Bay which leads into Holly Days and by the time Fish Creek Winter Games hit, we've come full circle. We've learned not to do the dinner out anytime from May through October. That's still the peak money-making time for everyone. Because I freelance I have more flex in my schedule. And I prefer to host in winter."

"How many members do you have in The Guild?" Melanie asked.

"Twelve--a mixed dozen, I call it. The personalities are so varied, but over time we've discovered we have more in common than books and food." Kate continued, "I hope you won't mind, but I'm hosting this evening and I have to keep an eye on the special dinner I've been cooking up for the girls--Pork Tenderloin with my Special Caribbean Cream Sauce. We've cooked up everything from soups and salads to desserts, using a lot of recipes from Jeanne Larson Hyde's cookbook, *Hazel's Kitchen Table* or *Cooking in Door County* by Pauli Wanderer. It's really up to each hostess," she explained.

"And you're the hostess chosen to kick off the anniversary year?"

That's part of it. "One of the honors associated with being Madame President. You know Melanie, you're going to end up with some great recipes by the time we're done with this interview. The members decided we could create an excellent cookbook, so we published one. I'll give you a copy before you leave today. Some of the recipes are Door County specialties and then there are some wonderful surprises, like Hannah's Matzos Cake. Hannah is a treasure. At eighty-three she continues to amaze us. She had belonged for years to another club before she moved here and joined the Guild. Once in a while she shares things from the journal she started as a young bride."

HANNAH VILAS

February Journal Entries
by
Edith Nash

February 28, 1998:

5:40 p.m.   Cooked an egg roll in new stove. Voice on the radio is Garrison Keillor's--light, feminine, really different from previous persona. The fire blazing warmed the glass house--an appropriate welcome mat on this clear, cold February night. But the glass windows appear too revealing. My reflection isolated--lonely.

After living in the Nation's Capital, moving to Central Wisconsin, now settled in Door. Joined a Literary group almost a year ago. Will it end up like all the other clubs? Sharing my journal entries from years passed with the group has served as a means of introducing myself to all of them.

February 1990: Notes about the 18th Century Club

As the Seine splits Paris, the river splits this cozy Midwest town. I came here years ago visiting my husband's hometown. Me, a young wife with a new baby --Magdalena was maybe 3 months old?   I put her down on a big double bed upstairs at someone else's house during my first club meeting. "Such a beautiful baby !" everyone would say.

My mother-in-law was a founding member of the 18th Century Club established in 1900. My husband's family were pioneers in lumbering, and in building dams on the great river. Mine were immigrant Jews, escaping conscription in the German army of 1850, now established in business: agriculture in California, and merchandising and advertising in Chicago.

My mother and father were married in Chicago, at Jenkin Lloyd Jones' church, called All Souls. These two couples, culturally so different from one another, turned out to be very similar in many ways.

Both of my parents were culture-freaks; my father an autodidact and my mother a student at the fledgling University of Chicago. My father read the 13th edition of the Encyclopedia Britannica for pleasure. And my mother, less genuinely a knowledge-seeker, but more of an activist, was a member of the Women's International League for Peace and Freedom. My husband's family read Dickens at Christmastime and had a collection of 18th Century women writers. My brother and I read Freud and Black poets: Countee Cullen and Langston Hughes.

My mother-in-law was very accepting of me as her adored son's wife. I always thought she was grateful to me for validating her son's masculinity by marrying him and bearing his children. She must have known she had taken up his love life from birth to late adolescence with her passion for music, the world of performance and city lights--her window to the BIG WORLD.

I visited the club then, and after we moved to the

6

town they decided to ask me to join. "She's a brain," they said. I was glad to do so. It pleased my mother-in-law and gave me at least one day a month away from the mundane household duties, two babies and all the dreariness. The club members took trips to various countries and gave term papers on the countries they visited. Sometimes these were based on fact, but more often they were pure fantasies.

The meetings included a ladies' lunch--the best silver, dishes and linens were gotten out. One or two maids served food made by experts of the community. Some cooked themselves. A favorite dish was homemade cream puffs with creamed chicken.

When my husband, Karl, was a little boy he used to sit on the stairs when the club met at his house. Waiting for the luncheon to be served, so he could go to the kitchen and eat one of those unctuous, delicious chicken a la kings. He sat at the kitchen table while the maids ran in and out the swinging door; bringing rolls, coffee, and peas. For dessert there was ice cream--homemade-- turned from the White Mountain freezer. Ice cream was made from a rich, custard base flavored with vanilla and a touch of almond. His favorite was peach, if peaches were available from Michigan.

Years ago in Washington, D.C. I went to a dinner party at the old Kennedy-Warren Hotel where some expatriates from Wisconsin were entertaining their aging parents and some friends. I walked into the dining room of the apartment and was astonished to see the table. This was the era of buffet service, bamboo trays, stainless steel and informal dining, about 1960. Instead I encountered an ironed, white tablecloth and napkins; shined, real silver; cups and saucers in place that matched the dinner china; and glasses with ice water. Two maids served. "I bet you were raised in Central Wisconsin," I said to the hostess and she agreed. Her husband was, and she had always tried to preserve the ambience of his home. The dinner was somewhat like Toronto custom, where we lived around 1940--"a joint, two veg and a pudding" was the mantra of that time. And ice cream and cake for dessert. Probably angel food. We had lived in Washington for two stints in the federal government. I founded and ran a school there.

When we returned to Wisconsin and the cranberry business in 1978 I happily returned to the 18th Century Club. Changes had taken place and I was surprised by the excellence of the programs. The first one involved a book review of a history of the UAW and the three Reuther brothers, their influences on Soviet methods of manufacture, and Victor's injuries at the hands of Ford's goons. Another was on the Bill of Rights, and several were on artists of opera, concert stage, and Broadway theater. Although members were loyal Republicans, (mostly Kohler Republicans rather than McCarthy Republicans, though some older members were close to McCarthy during his fiery heyday) these papers were presented carefully, and a-politically. I was astonished at how different it seemed compared to my memory of it from earlier times. Maybe I had changed as much as they, I had wondered.

Back in Wisconsin I had thrown myself into the club--planning meals when it was my turn to entertain, that went with the subject matter of the paper to be presented. One lunch I remember serving Julia Child's chicken with red and green peppers, cooked in a gold pan. For some reason, that dish went with my review of two books about Margaret Mead--Jane Howard's *Margaret Mead: A Life* and Cathy Bateson's *With A Daughter's Eye* about both her parents--Margaret Mead and Gregory Bateson.

My household helpers are two remarkable women who clean my house once a week--"the lunch bunch" as my husband, Karl called them--because I planned lavish and inventive lunches for these women.

My two helpers came to serve, but not in uniform. Once we had a salad buffet where each club guest made her own, but usually it was served at the table. I had wanted to do a fondue one time, but the idea was abandoned. Other members thought the fires might be too hazardous for the elderly.

I recall, too, that all the windows would be washed on Club Day. This always reminds me of the Jewish custom of searching the house for chametz before Passover; to clean out any leaven. Matzos are baked without leaven in memory of the Exodus from Egypt.

New members were proposed by any member, and the by-laws, which were seldom read, said they should be proposed at one meeting and voted on when the group met again. Voting was by secret ballot, just yes or no. If as many as three nos were recorded, the proposed member was not invited to join.

During the long years of our residing elsewhere, a best friend of someone in the club was rejected for membership. Reverberations reached all the way to Washington. In protest, there were threats to resign; recriminations and tantrums. But life went on. By the time I returned in the 70's, the proposals were handled more politically. The person proposing a new member phoned each member in advance; described the candidate; and "sold" her to the other members. As the world changed it became harder to attract new members. Often the proposed members were entirely unknown to me. I figured if a member knew the person and liked them, they were O.K. with me. I always voted "yes" and thought most of the others did too.

Then I brought this young woman to a program as a guest. Several people commented, " She would be a good member." So, I did not call everyone to clear the proposal. I thought this maneuver unnecessary. No one told me my candidate had been rejected. I returned from time away and was thinking of calling my friend to welcome her into the club when a neighbor casually dropped the information that the young woman had been rejected. I raged, accused, explained and then resigned from the club. What nonsense! I felt it was a rejection of me, since my candidate had no negative characteristics. And all the negatives I had heard about the club surfaced. My then grown children could not understand why I would belong to such an organization with its exclusionary by-laws and practices.

The day after I resigned, two club members called on me. The President, a most attractive young woman-- organized and intelligent. She was accompanied by the guardian of the Victorian period. This delegation wanted me to reconsider. "Don't you like us anymore ?" one said. Another member sent a dozen red roses and these were truly admired. I suggested it was time to revise the by-laws and it was time to appoint a study group to recommend changes, especially in the black-balling procedure.

I was about to ask them to discuss rescinding the rejection of my friend as a condition of my returning to membership, and then the phone rang. I talked to the person who called and when I returned to the living room my messengers had their coats on and were leaving. The young President whispered, "I couldn't do anything." And out the door they went.

I see several of the members of the club at lunch or at some other events, but have not really missed the club meetings. My obsession with menu planning is redirected toward our family's entertaining--the Fourth of July, Thanksgiving, Christmas Eve, St. Patrick's Day, Seder at the beginning of Passover and other occasions of celebration.

April 1995: Notes from Hannah's Journal

I wasn't prepared for the death of Karl.   I remember thinking, *What will I do now?   Stay in Central Wisconsin?   Returning to Washington isn't even an option.   I have always found peace in my visits to Door County--and money is not a problem.   I think I will go for a long weekend after the memorial service.*

April 1996: Notes from Hannah's Journal

Time for reflection.   REMEMERING THE POTLUCK: The master of ceremonies at the service invited everyone to the house . . . and they all came!   I recall Karl saying, "You don't get to be my size by trifling with food or drink."

First, raw meat, brought by the neighborhood hunter --a woman who prowls the yards at night with her gun to destroy her garden enemies--rabbits, raccoons, ground hogs or squirrels.   The carefully chopped meat was piled high in the middle of the platter, surrounded by little excremental piles of onion, capers, anchovies and red and green peppers.

11

Next, our smoothest friends brought a liver pate, chopped by machine to a creamy paste.

Their faces, both man and wife, were made up for television, since they were always being seen. They said soft words to me and my daughters, the bereaved. I was wearing a new green, wool dress. My daughters were in dance tights, draped with Native American jewelry, in honor of their father, the Great White Father.

The green salad was beautiful, composed by one who had seen her salad days. A daughter said, "This is not a bunch of hot dishes; this is real food."

Some guests moved to the porch for gin, whiskey, and rum. Wasps had built a nest just outside as the preacher's family looked for cranberry punch, the color of blood.

"You don't sit shiva anymore, do you?"

" I never did. But I wished I had." The mourner sits on a low stool; has food brought to her; does no work. All the members of the community hold her and her children in their loving suspension. No chatter. No distraction. No chirping.

A shifty-looking person brought a jello ring. A chocoholic brought brownies. The flatulent brought beans. The couple with new and ill-fitting dentures brought pasta salad, al dente.

Everyone chirped liked birds; sashayed like ducks; were proud like lions; gaggled like geese; mourned like doves; boasted like bantam roosters (Rhode Island Reds), and sang a loony tune.

February 1997: Notes from Hannah's Journal
Six months in Sturgeon Bay, my new home. I'm excited about joining the oldest book club in Door County. The

Door County Literary Guild is a wonderful, colorful mix of women. Anyone being rejected from this group is inconceivable. Me and Jerralyn, Anna, Edie, Emmi, Amanda, Inge, Kate, Gail, Louise, Sally and of course, Beverly.

February Journal Entries

BEVERLY THIEL

A *March Madness*
by
Justin Isherwood

Beverly knew, as every Door County native knew, that March is the loneliest month. And everyone on the lake side knew better than those who dwelt inland or on the bay; how the wind, cold enough in winter, seemed ever colder now with the promise of spring. It was this temperament of the Door that kept civilization away so effectively. Harried Chicago and Milwaukee outlanders invaded every summer, fall and winter, but they weren't here in March when the on-shore winds piled the rotten ice from the wide lake in great ruined walls.

What Beverly Thiel, 69, found interesting with Jacksonport's lake shore was what every beachcomber equally sought . . . beguiling junk. It pleased her to wander the shore after a hard Noreaster. Ramble along the frozen shards, to see what trash had washed up what was lodged between chunks of ice the size of freight cars. This is how it happened that she found Henry the Second.

15

Twenty-eight or thirty, she guessed. *Hair, yet blonde and abundant. Probably Scandinavian. Five foot ten with good hands and almost hairless chest.* He was blue-eyed and quite naked when she found him on the frozen beach dune. Stuck on the ice jam, encased in a crystal sarcophagus and very dead. He looked strangely familiar.

In all probability blown overboard during a late voyage the previous autumn. There were reports in the <u>Green Bay Press Gazette</u> and the <u>Door County Advocate</u> of several deck hands lost from ships of foreign registry. Most authorities presumed they had simply jumped ship hoping to immigrate. It was so much easier for the ship's company to claim them lost at sea than file a report of immigrancy violation.

Naked as a nail she found him. Eyes open, mouth frozen into a slight grimace. Not that it took him long to die, the lake water cold as always.

Slavic maybe? Polish? Hungarian? Definitely hung-something. Beverly giggled at her rude thought. *Michaelangelo's David wasn't the same caliber at all compared to this crystallized man.*

She found him on the shore near her modest house under the bluff. Poor fellow, frozen in clear ice, immobilized; entombed in a pose considered heroic by the Greeks.

Beverly had heard stories about men when they die-- in the process of dying, ejaculate one last time. *Curious,* she thought. *Why should that occur? Maybe it's just Nature or God being kind.* The gross thought bothered her, raised a Lutheran she had always kept carnal thoughts at a distance. Never mind the delicious rumors of what Methodist women did to keep their men content.

16

Henry the First, bless his heart, had to take her as she was when it came to sex . . . nothing acrobatic. No optional equipment. No exploration. Not once in the late night dream, did Beverly try what the dream said to try. Henry, knowing his part, never asked, for which she was grateful. Beverly never knew and never asked if he went to Kangaroo Lake to sample the brothel rumored to operate in that woods, featuring girls from Chicago. None of them Lutheran.

Why she suddenly had these thoughts she did not know, but then finding a naked man on the beach, a dead and naked man whose penis stood out from him can cause a widow woman to have divergent thoughts. It was, after all, a pose no public gallery ever dared. A pose that wasn't so much well hung as well elevated.

Beverly knew the legal procedures for reporting a body. Twenty years previous, she had discovered a child washed ashore, poor sodden thing. She called the sheriff's department at Sturgeon Bay and they sent up a coroner and ambulance and within a few hours they were done and gone. Bodies often came ashore here in bays and harbors of the northern Door. Fisherman drown and land currents carry them north along the shoreline. Bodies had been found for years all along the peninsula . . . on the shore of Green Bay, Baileys Harbor, Moonlight Bay and Gills Rock. This was, after all, part of the same peninsula that, at its tip, is the strait known as Death's Door. Named by the Native Americans and translated from French traders "Portes des Morts", it hit Beverly close to home today.

As said, she knew the right thing to do. The sheriff's phone number was on the cupboard door, same with the hospital number; it did suprise her how the paper had

17

yellowed. A phone number kept ever handy since the day they learned Henry the First had a bad heart. Not that any of the numbers saved him. Somehow she wasn't prepared to be a widow at 52. He was dead in less than three minutes; she, a widow now 17 years. Retired from teaching at the Gibraltar system three years ago, tending her house on the shore, walking her dog, potting her flowers, always the deep wish that her man hadn't died. Even wishing sometimes she was a little less Lutheran.

She ought to call the sheriff's department, they'd have the body out in a couple of hours. Probably wouldn't even ask her any questions. She really ought not to have touched it in the first place and felt how smooth he was--how perfectly smooth. And she should not have gone back and gotten her four wheel drive ATV with the leaf cart and wormed her way down to the body of Henry II. She shouldn't have chopped the blond man loose from the ice and slid him onto the cart; tying him aboard with rubber bungee straps. She had never tied a man down before. Especially one who looked so . . . so useful. It was rather macabre but she, for some reason, didn't care. Then she remembered Faulkner's *A Rose for Emily.* She understood something the literature class back at Gibraltar couldn't possibly understand. That a woman widowed at 52 years still has dreams, dreams Lutherans can't talk about. Things she didn't dare even with the one person she loved with all her heart. In her worst moments she wished all Lutherans be damned, especially those shriveled hypocrites of the cloth who interposed something impermeable and cruel between her and Henry.

She really ought to have called the sheriff instead of

18

taking the body of the unfortunate up the winding bluff trail, the ATV in low gear . . . taking him home. She thought he, Henry the Second needed something, some moment, in a living room, in a kitchen, soup on the stove, candles on the table . . . before the authorities came and summarily bagged him and laid him out on a stainless steel drawer. The church would never understand. She should have called the sheriff instead of dragging him, actually he slid quite easily, into the corner of the kitchen--where she, with some significant effort, stood him up. The icy countenance slid repeatedly back to the floor. It was like trying to make an icicle stand. Finally she got a rubber mat under him and that kept him upright.

Then Beverly prepared a hearty soup with potatoes, onions, milk and garlic. Served it up with rye bread. Then she remembered the bottle of champagne in the basement. She forgot why it was there? Oh yes, that was the bottle she and Henry bought to celebrate their wedding anniversary. An anniversary they never got to.

The following day, at noon, she called the sheriff and reported a body on the shore. The coroner came up with his big Dodge 4 X 4, drove the truck down to the beach and took some pictures, then bagged the man. How they roughly shoved him in the zippered shroud. Like the stovewood they slid him onto the back of the truck.

The coroner appeared puzzled and just before leaving, walked over to Beverly to thank her for reporting the death. They fell into an uneasy conversation about the time of discovery, the body's location . . . then he remarked how strange it was. He had seen many other like deaths, killed by similar circumstances.

Almost always, they were the same, he said. How strange this Mister John Doe wasn't, you know . . . erect . . . especially given his age and considering his youthful physique.

Beverly must have looked curious when he said the word, erect. She blushed and the coroner quickly apologized for his too candid remarks.

He went on with his observations almost absent-minded. Usually the eyes are frozen open as well; this one has a serene look you don't often see at death. *He, Mister Doe, looks way too satisfied--dying the way he did.* Usually the lake leaves them with a look of terror frozen on their face, still he mused, the lake does funny things. It was a question Beverly could have answered in some detail.

They passed small talk for awhile, she invited him up for a cup of coffee and a bit of lunch.

I don't mean to trouble you, he said.

No trouble, she said. I've a nice pot of potato chowder on the stove. The floor's been mopped and tonight my book club members won't arrive before six.

He laughed at that and opened the door for her. On the passenger side the white letters "County Coroner" were sprawled across the panel.

I hope you like potato soup with rye bread, she said.

He smiled back at her. It was a good day to be overwhelmed by soup.

ANNA PEDERSON

April Surprise
by
Barbara Fitz Vroman

"*It's May! It's May! The merry month of May!*"
All day the phrase from a Camelot song kept barging into
Anna's head. Her window framed the steel needles of rain
drilling down from a dead, drab April sky.

Anna notices Emil Simonsen walking his dog. He
always used to wave to her. He no longer waves. She
feels the familiar welling of sadness. Resolutely, she
forces her mind back to the party that night. She was
supposed to have had The Door County Literary Guild in
May, but Sally Applebach had to go to Chicago because
her sister became ill, and the club president, Kate Murphy
asked Anna to switch.

"Are you sure you're up to it?" Inge, one of the
Guild's early bird, asked with a worried look. Anna said
she was sure it would be all right. Actually, she hadn't
felt well all day. The truth was, she was disappointed.

Anna was ashamed of her bare bones farm house.
The living room wallpaper had grown brown with age.

21

The wood floor in the kitchen was worn into a dip in front of the old sink. And the knobby woodwork was layered with paint. Whenever she thought of Hannah's beautiful new house with all that glass--windows opening up the entire front view looking out over Green Bay with ruby rugs and fine art displayed on the walls--or Edie's gracious Victorian, an old bed and breakfast inn, which was featured in <u>MidWest Living</u> magazine last summer, she could kick herself for switching with Sally. She had counted on hosting in May. The old, blue house being flooded with cherry blossoms and the newly washed, lace curtains breathing the fresh air--in and out--with the sweet scent of a Door County spring.

Instead, here she was stuck with T.S. Eliot's "April is the cruelest month." Damp, chilly, and grey. But her mother, who had lived in the same house before her, had taught her to make the most of things.

"We have music," her mother would say. The old upright piano in the room called out to be played. "We have cleanliness." Oh yes, Anna had cleanliness. She had scrubbed until . . . well, until all the twinges pulsed in her back, but she wasn't going to worry about that. Not tonight. Tonight was too important. "AND do we have BOOKS!" We have many books! They surround the walls of the library which also houses the piano.

It was the love of books that had brought all these women into her life in the first place. And FOOD. Anna tended to think of everything in terms of food. She wasn't sure if this was because she weighed 300 pounds, or if she weighed 300 pounds because she was such a good cook. Besides she had absolutely no will power. Always the pleaser. Anna never wanting to rock the boat, or disappoint--anyone.

As she sifted the flour and beat the eggs for the cake she was making for tonight's meeting, she reflected that members of the club were like the ingredients.

Hannah and Beverly were the sugar with their large, kind hearts. Beverly baked food for church suppers, and read to the Scandia Nursing Home residents in Sister Bay. She liked everything that M. Scott Peck and Rabbi Harold Kushner wrote.

Hannah had traveled widely, lived in elite Washington society and had learned to cook in Paris. She educated the members on Jewish traditions and gourmet cooking.

Jerralyn and Gail were the eggs in the recipe. Each in her own way frothed and leavened the ingredients with their humor.

Gail had a deadpan humor that often made her travel adventures sound hilarious. She enjoyed books by P.D. Wodehouse.

Tall and thin, Jerralyn was an international singing star, but her down-to-earth manner welcomed each of them. She was very inventive in her storytelling. When she read, the members laughed themselves out of their chairs.

Anna thought of Kate as the milk in the recipe. A writer and photographer, her vitality and creativeness were as nourishing as milk to the rest of them. She enjoyed fun books and writers that like to play with words. She presented books by Clyde Edgerton, Tom Robbins, and John Irving. She also brought to the Guild's attention books unique to Door County, like Norb Blei's *Door Way* or *Fish Creek Voices* by Ed and Lois Schreiber. And she'd announce classes being held at The Clearing in Ellison Bay or Peninsula Art School in Fish Creek. A list of Door County books was available at Passtimes Books in Sister

Bay or she would talk with the owner of Wm. Caxton Books in Ellison Bay. Her own library housed every book she could get her hands on that was written by a Wisconsin writer.

Sally was the salt. Anna had not liked her at first. She was so quick, and critical. But over time she had come to value this strong, honest woman. Underneath her saltiness was a brain so lively; a loyalty once won so supreme; and an insight so deep that Anna would have parted from most members of the group, except her.

Emmi had bright dark eyes and a Gypsy laugh. Besides reading Tarot cards she could be found dancing in the moonlight. Anna decided long ago that Emmi was definitely the spice in the cake. Emmi introduced the guild to poetry books, including her own, and ways of using everyday things that made them magical.

Amanda and Edie were the baking powder. Divorcees, both raised the consciousness of the group with books by Germaine Greer, Betty Friedan and Gloria Steinem. Amanda was the one who taught the group about art.

Inge, a delightful woman, provided flavorful vanilla. German with a sweetness of spirit, Inge loved travel logs and photography. She, Gail, Kate and Hannah compared numerous adventures.

Anna thought of herself as the flour. Bland, heavy, but still a necessary ingredient that bonded all the other ingredients together. It was Anna, the youngest of a large family, who stayed ungrudgingly to care for her mother in her last days. She was the one who was most available to all the others. It was Anna who somehow mitigated any quarrels and who led the group back to the old classics that still resided on her mother's worn bookshelves . . . Dickens, Chekhov, Victor Hugo.

"Well, folded together we all make a wonderful cake," Anna talked to herself as she rubbed one last coat of paste wax into the old oak table so it would glow. One hand against her back to halt the twinges.

She straightened and surveyed the house with pleasure in spite of the drawbacks. Bereft of cherry blossoms, she had played with the idea of buying flowers. But, that was beyond her scant budget. Instead she had used candles. The wonderful, fat, fragrant candles she made to sell in Door County gift shops. Beautiful colors of claret, cranberry, sage and blueberry. The candles supplemented her tiny wage as assistant librarian and it gave her a creative outlet. Now, she placed her mother's kerosene lamp in the center of the oak table. She had electricity but liked the pool of light the lamp spilled onto the table. It had grown dark enough to light the lamp and the candles. In a few minutes the first ladies would be arriving.

Anna peered out the window and was glad to see the rain had stopped. It was as dark as a midnight closet. She lit the candles on the piano. In the kitchen she opened one of the windows just enough to let the wet-earth-leaf-rain smell seep into the house and mingle with the essence of vanilla, cranberry and sage.

In the final minutes before everyone arrived, Anna shoved her dented coffee pot onto the flame of the gas stove. They wouldn't be drinking coffee until later, but she wanted the aroma to greet them along with the fragrance of fresh baked bread. All of this would make up for the scrubbiness of her little farm house.

She pulled the cracked shades and drew the lace curtains in the living room. Alone, she never used the shades. She loved bare windows. On spring days she

25

watched Emil as he drove his tractor back and forth in his fields while white sea gulls hovered over him. The gulls waited for the dark soil to be turned, insects became exposed and they could feast upon them. In June, from the west window, there was a view of red roses growing along the old stone wall. From the west she could also catch a glimpse of the white church steeple six miles away in Ephraim. At night the windows gave her star shine and moonlight.

Ah, her windows. Every night Anna thanked God for the beauty outside in every season. She could no longer kneel at the bed to say her prayers as she had done when she was a child, but she felt that God understood. Believed that God understood about a great many things that other people might condemn her for.

Then Jerralyn arrived, usually one of the first, as Anna knew she would. Jerralyn's cheek, rain-misted, pressed cool against hers for a moment.

"Are you all right, darling Anna?" she asked.

"I'm doing fine," Anna assured her. At that minute she did feel fine. Her famous pound cake had turned out perfectly. The house, bathed in candlelight, would do and all her wonderful friends were arriving one by one.

Hannah usually arrived last and when she did, everyone settled into their place in the parlor. The women looked at each other with happiness and anticipation and the meeting began.

Anna found her usual concentration was disturbed by her duties as hostess. Ten minutes before the mid-evening break, she slipped away to take the bread from the oven so it could cool enough for slicing.

She had just lifted the golden loaf out when it happened. A soft, swooshing sound and suddenly she

26

stood in a pool of water. She could not help the high-pitched cry that issued from her lips.

Inge instantly ran into the kitchen. "Oh, Lord!" she called out. Six other faces bobbed in the doorway. Inge turned and shouted to the others, "Call the hospital !!! Anna's having a baby!"

Beverly rolled her eyes toward the top of her head. Louise exclaimed, " But Anna's never been with a man in her life!" Gail couldn't resist saying, "I don't think this is the second immaculate conception, do you?" Stunned, Amanda asked the question they all wanted the answer to, "Why didn't you tell us?"

"I was . . . embarrassed," Anna said before another intense contraction interrupted her. She grunted, "I did tell Sally."

That was the end of the inquisition and any condemnation. The other women leapt into action. Louise called the Emergency Room and then went to get a nightie and toiletries. Emmi offered her van and ran out to arrange a sleeping bag in the back. Jerralyn and Edie went throughout the house to blow out the candles. Everyone of them decided they would be there for Anna.

Emmi came back in and announced, "The van is ready. Let's go!"

It took six of them to get Anna moved to the back of the van. Propped up on two pillows, with Beverly holding one hand, and Edie timing the contractions. Anna was in pain, but never so happy.

For months, Anna had worried, *How am I going to raise this child--alone?* Now looking out the back window of the van, she saw the long row of golden headlights that followed her and knew she had nothing to fear.

27

April Surprise

28

SALLY APPLEBACH

May Interlude
by
Marriann Ritzer

May, with all its promise, is still a complicated month. Tourists begin to trickle through Door on the weekends. Parking in front of restaurants and the shops becomes a major headache.

Trilliums, daffodils, tulips, crocuses battle for my undivided attention. The sun sends out occasional, warm hints of the summer ahead. The wind blows in from the Fish Creek beach warming me, chilling me. I'm here, but part of me is not. Part of me is worried about my banana cream pie; part of me is worried that the Literary Guild won't like my selection of the month.

The innkeeper has been helpful, but I'm still mad as hell. I called him months ago to reserve the <u>large</u> cottage for the weekend. When I drove in late last night and discovered he reserved the small one instead AND all the other cottages were booked, I lost it. "Shit!" I said. "How am I supposed to fit twelve people in this matchbox parlor?" With a look of utter desperation on my face, I threw my hands up in the air. Tears began to fall. My mascara ran in little, black rivers down my cheeks. But, I didn't tell him to go to hell or demand my money back or slam the door on my way out. I knew it took too much energy and I needed all my strength and my wits about me to make the pies and to deal with Anna's recent news. *Maybe she won't come tonight, but that still leaves me with the pies. Why didn't I just buy them at Perkins on my way up Interstate 43?*

If it were up to me, we'd all serve wine and cheese and sour cream dip with potato chips. *Maybe some white cheddar cheese popcorn, too.* Every time I've brought this up to the members, I've been voted down. Amanda is a recovering alcoholic with very little will power. The club voted to go alcohol-free to help her until she got stronger. I think three years is long enough.

The other problem is that Amanda is the granddaughter of the founder of the club. In deference to her lineage (waitresses have no lineage) the club members continue to cater to her whims. And if she is in Door, she never misses a meeting. I always stash a little wine and cheese and chips (enough for eleven) in the trunk of my car, just in case Amanda is in Colorado or traveling somewhere else. And when the expiration dates on the products in my trunk get close, Thad and I throw a party.

I love Thadius. He's the reason I'm in the book club. Excuse me. I should have said, The Door County Literary Guild. His parents owned a small engine repair shop just off Highway 57 in Baileys Harbor. When they retired, they turned the business and ten acres of land over to Thad.

One warm August night about six years ago I was having drinks with friends at the Top Deck and watching the sun set over North Bay. At the time I was dabbling in real estate, looking for a new career, hating my life. Thad and I started talking; one thing led to another. I became his broker and his lover. I moved in with him in his family's home until I sold it for him. Then I moved back to Milwaukee with him and we've been carrying on ever since.

After the move I grew so homesick for Door County. I'd spent a majority of my adult life waiting on tables up and down the peninsula. Even did one summer at Al Johnson's Swedish Restaurant in Sister Bay. But the manager I worked with was too bossy for my personality, so I moved on. Besides, I hated those awful Swedish uniforms we had to wear. But the *coup de grace* happened the night I decided to sleep on the grass roof with the goats. Gunner, the manager, didn't have a sense of humor in those days.

What all this has to do with the club is that Thad's mother belonged to it. She dropped a note to Thad saying the club was looking for a new member and that they needed someone with long-time ties to Door County. With my passion for reading and my waitress-apron strings tied to the County, I was voted in.

That's what brings me to this tiny cottage in Fish Creek. I'm getting ready to host this month's meeting. The innkeeper said he'd round up some chairs. Those chairs along with the wicker sofa, plus the chair in the tiny parlor and the four in the equally-tiny dining room should suffice.

I have slept until almost eight this morning. The night before, the small bedroom encircled me as if I were

31

wrapped in a full-size, down-filled comforter. Through the partially-opened narrow window, the swaying of the giant cedars lulled me to sleep. But I woke up at midnight dreaming I had burned the meringue on the pies. I'm an awful baker, but I have to have a banana cream pie to go with my book of the month selection.

I had thought of choosing Annie Ernaux's *Simple Passion* for May and then decided against it for two reasons: Ernaux is French. Any French recipe would be too complicated for me. The other reason is that the book is about a woman who has an affair with a married man. It's all about obsession and deceit. And the guy leaves her in the end and the woman is left with nothing but her journal of memories. For a whole year she did nothing else but wait for her man to come. She actually counted the times they'd made love.

This story is too much like what Kate's life must be like, the life she is trying to keep secret. But nothing's secret for very long in these small coastal villages on Highways 42 and 57. From Egg Harbor to Gills Rock, people know about your affairs before you do. Even though I only get up to Door once a month now, I still hear everything when I stop at the Bayside Tavern in Fish Creek, or visit the AC Tap or, of course, have a cup of coffee at Al's. But I don't stop there unless Gunner is on vacation. Some Swedes can carry grudges.

So, in order to spare Kate any embarrassment, I've stayed clear of any discussions about indiscretions or affairs. And to save myself from any embarrassment, I've stayed away from French cooking. Banana cream pie will be hard enough for me to pull off. But I have my mother's foolproof recipe. The secret to a great banana cream pie is in the custard. You make it from scratch in a double boiler; you never buy the instant pudding and pie mix, although it would have been easier on me, if I did. The other secret is the meringue. Never substitute with a whipped cream. The custard and the meringue whirl your taste buds into a passionate frenzy that turns out to be the key ingredient to enjoying my selection for the book club, *What We Carry* by Dorianne Laux. The love poems are in the last part of the book. These poems have nothing to do with affairs. They have everything to do with love: married love, some "before-marriage" love--but no "during-marriage" love affairs.

While I stir the custard in the double boiler, waiting for the ingredients to thicken, I read again the first part of a truly great love poem by Laux called, "This Close."

> In the room where we lie, light
> stains the drawn shades yellow.
> We sweat and pull at each other, climb
> with our fingers the slippery ladders of rib.
> Wherever our bodies touch, the flesh
> comes alive. Heat and need, like invisible
> animals, gnaw at my breasts, the soft
> insides of your thighs. What I want
> I simply reach out and take, no delicacy now,
> the dark human bread I eat handful
> by greedy handful . . .

The custard has thickened. It is ready. And so am I. Suddenly I need a drink stronger than the wine in the trunk of my car. I run down to The Bayside for a quick shot of anything to calm my urges. Who should be sitting at the bar, sipping on a brew, but Alaska Jack.

"My god ! Alaska ! What are you doing here?" I pull up a stool next to him. He smiles, looks at me with his great blue eyes as if no time has passed, as if we had just seen each other this morning.

"Hey Sal," he says. "God, you're looking good."

I order a Bloody Mary with a Miller Lite chaser. Before I met Thad six years ago, Alaska and I had a pretty good thing going. He was staying in the County to take care of his aging mother who lived in Fish Creek. She got worse and they moved her to the nursing home in Sister Bay. Alaska stayed on, living in the homestead and visited his mother regularly. I stayed with Alaska and helped him through this difficult time. We were a pair made in heaven. Our bodies fit together, whether walking or making love. His tongue and hands knew the canyons of my body and I knew the depths of his soul. We were beautiful together. Then the reason he came back to Door evaporated; his mother died. He had dealt with her affairs and returned to Alaska. Late that August I had moved on to Thad.

Alaska and I talk about old times now while we finish our drinks. One thing leads to another and pretty soon we are back at the cottage with the cooling custard. He watches while I blend the custard with the bananas in the pie shell. I still have three hours before the members arrive. "I think I'll wait on the meringue," I say to him. "Plenty of time for that." I finish reading to him the poem that sent me out of the cottage in the first place.

> . . . *Eyes, fingers, mouths,*
> *sweet leeches of desire. Crazy woman,*
> *her brain full of bees, see how her palms curl*
> *into fists and beat the pillow senseless.*

*And when my body finally gives in to it
then pulls itself away, salt-laced
and arched with its final ache, I am
so grateful I would give you anything, anything.*

We run to the tiny bedroom. The antique double bed groans with our every move. We haven't changed a bit; we remember everything about each other's bodies, each other's passions. We fall asleep, having used it all up.

When I finally open my eyes again, it is five o'clock. "My god! The meringue !" I jump off the bed. "Last night I dreamt I burned it and ruined the pies! You've got to get out of here, Alaska. The women will be here in an hour!"

Alaska laughs his patient, sweet laugh. We collect our clothes and take them to the parlor to dress. The bedroom is only big enough for the bed, the dresser, a small round bedside table and armour. I quickly use the bathroom and then turn it over to Alaska. While he washes up, I go to the kitchen and begin gathering the ingredients for the meringue. *I will not burn it,* I say to myself. *I will not burn it this time. Only in my dreams. Only in my dreams.*

There is a knock on the door. I finish separating the egg whites from the yolks, wipe my hands on my jeans and answer the door. "Amanda ! It can't be six o'clock, can it? I'm still working on the meringue."

"I'm early, for a change. But don't worry, you've got plenty of time. Maybe I can help. I can't believe you got this tiny cottage. Do you think we'll all fit in here?" She's standing in the dining room, looking at the tiny parlor when Alaska walks out of the bathroom. "Jack?" she says. Then repeats in disbelief, "Jack?"

Amanda looks at me, looks at Alaska, and focuses for a moment back on me. She screams and runs out the door, running into the arms of the other early arrival, Inge Mueller.

I burned the meringue. I never read the last line of the poem to Alaska--*If I loved you, being this close would kill me.* And I've never read any poetry to Thad.

When people gossip they sometimes get the details mixed up. No one else knew about Kate until recently, but everyone knew that Amanda had an affair and that it resulted in a divorce. What we didn't know was that Amanda's affair wasn't with a married man; it was with Alaska Jack. With all my local connections, I hadn't heard he was back in town.

If I had known . . . no, I'm not going to lie . . . even if I'd known, I still would've done what I did this afternoon. I'm willing to take chances for the pure pleasure of getting from <u>here</u> to <u>there</u>. Because once you get <u>there</u>; life tastes so much better.

May is a complicated month.

EDIE SUMMERS

The June Dinner Party
by
Jackie Langetieg

The table is set for dinner. Edie stands with one hand against the door, looking at the beauty of the table knowing the true beauty of its symbolism.

What about the others, the eleven other members of the Guild? Can they get into the spirit of the evening-- look beyond old prejudices? She walks around the table, caressing the colorfully laminated placemat images that represent each of the twelve women. She has selected twelve women of historical importance. Each member will choose where to seat herself. Edie gives the room one more glance, carefully brings the doors together, enclosing the quietness of the room.

"I should have taken more time in cleaning . . . " she berates herself while walking through her large, sunny house. "No.no.no. I've had enough of that kind of ridiculousness--this is me. Take it or leave it!" Edie says

37

these things to herself each time she expects friends. Old habits die hard. She'd been a wife of the '50s--one of those slim, bouffant-haired, high-heeled women straightening a lace apron and waiting for the man of the house to share his day with her. This house truly reflects her. The men are gone, no more listening and comforting--except for herself. There's freedom here to pick up a book from the overflowing stacks. She wants the binoculars and books about trees in front of the window. If she had to run and look for them each time, she'd probably stop to pick up some lint from the rug, empty the cat litter or grab the vacuum.

The chime from the front door interrupts her ruminations. It's her son, Steven, with the fresh croissants he's bringing by for the dinner. "Steven, I'm glad you're here. Come in and take a look." Edie drags him into the dining room while the aroma of butter and yeast rises from the brown bags.

"There." Edie steps back and waits for Steven to comment. "What do you think?"

Steven looks at the lustrous image of the table, the settings emphasizing the grandeur of the Goddess Ishtar.

"It's that dyke art book, isn't it?"

"Still trying to get my goat?" Edie pokes him. "You've seen this. We've talked about it. I really want your reaction."

"What am I supposed to say, Mother? What difference does it make? It's your women friends you're really worried about."

"I'm not worried, just anxious. This subject is important and I don't want to lose anyone just because of the images."

"Okay, go ahead, practice on me."

"This is Ishtar," she begins, "mythic goddess, worshipped for thousands of years in Mesopotamia as the supreme giver and taker of life." Edie gestures toward the Ishtar placemat resting on an appliqued, embroidered runner. "The motifs are from the famous Ishtar Gate and the Ziggurat of Ur." Steven stands in silence still balancing the paper bags, which Edie now removes from his hands and places on the sideboard along the far end of the room. She'll add the coconut creamed vegetables, yellow rice and cabbage slaw with peanuts when the others have arrived. Orange sherbert and almond cookies will follow.

Steven moves toward the long table and is reading some of the place cards. "It's really sort of . . . neat, beautiful . . . I don't know." He looks a little confused. "It doesn't seem sexy or gay or whatever. It's okay, yeah. But I'd still like to see the look on weird Beverly's face when she sees it."

Edie sends him out the door, satisfied that what she saw in his face was more positive than negative. His remark about Beverly is right on target. *What if . . . no, no point at all in wondering.* We'll see soon enough, she tells herself as she walks through the living room.

The six foot tall candles in the corner set off the tableau of muscial instruments she collects; the guitar and Native American flutes have collected a bit of dust. She gives them a swipe with the feather duster she got at Sweet Basil in Egg Harbor. *There. None of that to dull your mahogany hides and dry your bodies.* She puts the duster on the floor by the guitar. The spicy aroma of the candles has given the room a delicious aura that should last the whole evening.

"Kali, my sleek feline of the underworld, you look too

comfortable, but company's coming. You'll have to give up that spot to one of my friends." The black cat, languishes on the back of the sofa. From her squinting, green eyes she slowly blinks a meaningful glance. Edie leans down and with a push of her nose, gives Kali a soft nudge. Kali answers back with a push of her own, closes her eyes, not for a minute admitting that she loves all these small gestures of special attention.

Edie paused in front of the gold-framed mirror in the foyer. "Oh, Kali. I love being old, but when did the Jowl Fairy pay a visit to my face." She looks sideways at her long, graying blond hair pulled cleanly back from a remarkably unlined face. "Oh well." She smiles back at her reflection. "In for an inch, in for a mile." And she does like the freedom of being older, even if her 60th this autumn seems an impossible age when she feels so young inside.

Her bedroom, itself, is a small library and craft shop with a table filled with watercolors, books, CD player, and more books. From their hangers, Edie pulls a long, white skirt and a crocheted, champagne-colored tunic top. She sheds her robe and sits down on the bed to put on her sandals. Kali jumps up and nuzzles her arm, asking for more attention. "Meeow," Kali coos to Edie and rolls over onto her back, presenting her soft stomach in trust. Edie strokes her rhythmically and then curls up next to her to rest--just for a minute, she tell herself.

She remembers joining the book club 15 years ago five years after she moved to Ellison Bay. Five hard years, adjusting from her divorce and moving away from family and friends. But it had been a fresh start and she'd soon felt her own strength. She supplemented her small, monthly income by writing. There were additional sales of the small handmade cards and paper novelties she made every winter to sell during the peak tourist trade of summer.

The poems had come fast and furiously to her in those years. She always wrote more when her life was in chaos. Her poems give her a little peace and serenity even when they eluded her. She'd written two novels as well. Even a bookseller at Passtimes Books in Sister Bay had made his way into one of her novels, becoming a sensual lover underneath his proper British reserve. Her next story featured the dissipated sailor at Ephraim who had taken her out on his small sailboat. He became a mercenary from wars of both soul and country and had given spice to her second novel. Her successes added a layer of new skin to her battered self.

When she first moved to Door County, she'd coveted an invitation to the Door County Literary Guild and was thrilled when the group decided to review her books. She'd smile at Gail Anderson, whom a friend had pointed out as the club's unofficial president, and Gail would smile back. After a year or so of running into each other at Door Community Auditorium events, they would stop and talk about writing, art, life, and changing times. Edie kept checking her mailbox for an invitation to join the Literary Guild, and finally one May morning, when the rain had nearly washed away the last of her resentments, Gail called and asked her to come to dinner for an evening with the book group.

The long-awaited invitation didn't seem quite so simple. Edie had spent a good part of her life enslaved to the opinion of others, competing with both women and men in social clubs and business dealings. Here, in the quiet of the winters and in the golden sunshine of the summers, she felt she'd finally shaken free and didn't want to lose herself again. Each morning at dawn, wearing a warm sweatshirt, she sat on the pier trying to get as far away from land as possible to ground herself in her own thoughts. As the light rose from the other side of the peninsula and opened the lake's darkness to soft grays, she'd meditate on her decision.

On Thursday, shivering after getting drenched in a shower, she decided she would try being part of a group again--a group of women. Now she could be objective about her role in it. She would give socializing another try.

Each meeting was unique. Sometimes, they did nothing more than pass the night's book around and then branch off into conversation. One time they laid on the grass in their own yards under a summer sky, watching as a meteor shower suffused them with streams of light. The next meeting they shared their feelings about the solitude of the experience.

Another time, they had told lightning stories following the book synopsis given from Gretel Ehrlich's *A Match to the Heart,* a book about being struck by lightning. Edie thought of that book as being the beginning of her own quest for her place in nature. She'd gone on to devour nonfiction books about women traveling, camping, communing with themselves and a greater truth. Last summer she took a trip to Montana for a week of camping with 50 other women who wrote, sang, danced, played musical instruments, filling the high meadows with their creative energies. The camp leader had talked about *The Dinner Party* and how she'd organized an 80-member woman's chorus to celebrate its emergence from the moth balls at Berkeley in 1996.

Edie silently repeats the names of all the book club members she can remember or has heard others talk about. They, too, are women of history, with their own accomplishments whether white-bread conservatives or seven grain strong, married, single, straight, gay, happy or sad.

"Meeeow," Kali jumps off the bed, and runs toward the hallway and the ringing doorbell. Edie quickly drops the skirt over her hips and pulls on the top. "Jerralyn and Inge always come early," she mutters to herself.

"*The Dinner Party*! I can't believe you've done this! Isn't this a lesbian theme?" Beverly says.

Edie takes a deep breath as she holds open the dining room doors while Jerralyn leads the others into the room.

"Don't be judgmental," Edie cautions. "We don't live in the 70's anymore. *The Dinner Party* is about women --we're about women. This will be fun, no false modesty or veiled embarrassment."

Edie moves candles onto the table for better illumination for her *tour de force*. She extends her invitation: "Everyone, just take a deep breath and look at it--the beauty of color. Walk around and look at each setting. Read the notes. You'll learn what another woman wants the world to know about women's history and who, if it matters, isn't a lesbian, just a woman artist."

Anna is the first to step forward, looking at the setting closest to her, "Hey, this is Virginia Woolf. Where did you get this idea?" Anna touches the print in front of her and reads aloud: "The incredible luminosity of her

43

writing is suggested by the painted and stitched light beam that emanates from beneath the plate."

Edie holds up the colorful book that explains the 1979 art exhibit, "This is the book for our June meeting, *The Dinner Party* by Judy Chicago. There was a revival of interest in 1996 when the work was brought out of storage at Berkeley. It's like opening a cornerstone 20 years later. Think of the furor this caused in the 70's. I know that I was embarrassed about the most private parts of womanhood, mine and everyone else's, spread out on a table, naked and opulent for all to see. I'd only heard about a woman's vagina or vulva from men telling jokes or from my doctor when I had my children."

Sally laughs conspiratorially as the women begin looking at the table. Each of the sculpted plates is the essence of a woman's body--a blending of a vulva or labial image with a free-form butterfly, brilliant colors and patterns reflecting the individuality of the woman represented. The white table covering is filled with names of more women she has carefully written to accompany each place setting. Edie straightens a napkin, itself a panel of information transferred by photocopy to cloth. She reads: "Virginia Woolf lived between 1882 and 1941." Edie goes on, "She was selected because she believed that the subjugation of women was the key to most of the social and psychological disorders of Western civilization. She felt that only if the so-called masculine and feminine traits were wed on all levels--emotional, intellectual and social--could the world be humanized."

Gail moves to the right of Anna looking at the elaborate panel for Emily Dickinson, the beautiful lace and netting, both eminently appropriate for this American Victorian lady. Gail introduces her chosen writing,

"Emily Dickinson supposedly said, 'I took my power in my hand and went out against the world.' It also says that the fierceness in her poetry was at odds with the prevailing ideas of what a woman of the time was supposed to be and do." Edie's anxiety about Gail fades with her obvious interest in Emily Dickinson. With the women moving around, showing interest on their own, Edie knows the evening will answer the promise she always knew was there.

Suddenly Emmi laughs and says to Gail, "This is fabulous. Did you know that Caroline Herschel taught herself mathematics by sheer force of will and was the first woman to discover a comet?"

"And look," says Beverly, "Eleanor of Aquitaine orgainzed 300 women to follow her on the Crusades. They were called the 'Queen's Amazons.' They wore coats of maile and tinted silk."

"But then her husband, King Henry the Second, put her in prison for 16 years, even though she'd supported him and helped solidify his power," Jerralyn breaks in, reading over her shoulder.

"After I put my husband through school, he left me for his boss' daughter," adds Amanda.

The ice broken, the women are animated and talking among themselves. Edie leans back against the doorway and smiles.

"When you've finished looking it over, help yourself to the food, then go to the place of the woman you most identify with or admire. Although I only have 12 here, there were 39 places in the actual setting. I don't think we'll have much duplication; I tried to select women who reflect our interests." Even as she moves toward the table and the place she has chosen, Edie wonders what the others are thinking about her and the chair she will sit in.

As the women settle into their seats, Edie introduces *The Dinner Party*, "The original work is an immense open table covered with fine white cloths set with 39 place settings, thirteen on a side, each commemorating a goddess, historic personage, or important woman. These settings include both vulva and butterfly motifs, the latter chosen in part because this is an ancient symbol of liberation." Edie looks up and says, "Butterflies are the metaphor for women's intensifying struggle for freedom." She tells them how the incorporation of vulva iconography in the context of *The Dinner Party* implies that these various women are represented though separated by culture, time, geography, experience and individual choices, and unified primarily by their gender, which, in the opinion of Chicago, is the main reason that so many were and are unknown. "Over 1,000 women are represented in the finished project, and the final completed piece opened at the San Francisco Museum of Modern Art in March 1979." Edie nods at the eleven women who are held in rapt attention. "Who wants to go on?"

Louise sits in front of the image of a naked woman lying on a bed, a stain of blood spread beneath her body. She has brushed her cheek several times, and her voice trembles as she begins to read from the page next to the plate: "This is Margaret Sanger, born in 1879 and died in 1966. As a nurse, she was confronted with endless pleas from women desperate for some form of birth control, which was entirely prohibited at the time. Then, in the year 1925, Sanger convened the first International Birth Congress, forerunner of today's Planned Parenthood."

Amanda is next to read; she introduces Sappho, then Beverly follows with Georgia O'Keeffe.

Each one takes a turn reading about the woman whose place they hold. They are reverent, then amused as one or another of them relates how their own lives exemplify the qualities of the woman they have chosen.

Edie strokes the blacks, browns, yellows of the runner under her plate; a pieced quilt that repeats the bold colors of a sculpted image and, when the others have finished, begins to speak again. "These woven bands in the runner are a pattern of African strip-weaving." Her voice is sure and strong. "The strips honor the efforts of the slave women to retain some vestige of their heritage. Although born into slavery in 1797, Sojourner Truth believed the liberation of blacks and that of women were closely related; she gave antislavery lectures that were infused with arguments for women's rights." Edie tells how Sojourner Truth changed her identity, her name and her position in life--from slave to defender of women. Truth was committed to her cause until her death at 86 in 1883. Edie places her hand gently on the words as she reads and knows she also has found the right spot at the table.

The crystal wind chime plays soft musical notes. The open patio doors invite the night into the room, and the scent of rich, pine spice mixes with the room's energy and warm feelings.

The June Dinner Party

LOUISE SORENSON

July - Birthday Memories
by
Kathleen Arnold

Louise decided to prepare a traditional Fish Boil for her friends from the Guild. Looking up the recipe brought back a flood of memories.

JULY. I don't know why I remember it so fondly or anticipate its coming each year. Maybe it's the residue of my childhood birthday parties. Swimming every day, slumber parties with my girlfriends as we all discovered boys. I remember swimming so long I'd want a warm shower. Even when it was 80 degrees outside, in the shower I would plan what a wonderful evening it would be. My parents' old friends were visiting from California. They brought their six children along as part of their summer vacation. A chance for new friends with no history or baggage. I was seven. Yes, life would be good this day.

1956. My eighth birthday month. There would be cards and presents from my grandparents. Many of those early birthdays were held at my grandparents home in Baileys Harbor. Mom and Dad had a few "well deserved" days at Kangaroo Lake. I developed friendships with grandma's neighbor kids. She'd let us sleep on the porch--our version of camping, instead of pitching a tent at Peninsula State Park. We'd laugh, giggle, snort until grandma's large silhouette appeared in the porch window. Hands on her hips and lips pursed, I knew we had crossed the Quiet Zone. But there was a little girl left in Grandma, too. As she would disappear and we would giggle again.

FOUR YEARS LATER. Summer 1960. If I didn't have to babysit my younger siblings, Grandma would drive us over to Egg Harbor and we'd spend the day at Murphy Beach. The neighborhood gang would discuss weekend plans. Maybe we'd go to a movie? We'd go over every detail--who we'd sit with; how many times we'd 'make-out.' Life was full of great expectations. Anticipation of possible love and other wonderful experiences consumed us.

1970. My wedding month. Now thinking back on it, I knew it was a mistake. I knew from the very beginning. An uneasy feeling, never quite being completely happy. Happiness comes when you see happiness in others. I don't think I ever made Joe completely happy either. We chose July to marry, honeymoon, and every year for 14 years we vacationed in Fish Creek. I, always hoping life would be better.

1979. The month I met Don. I'll never forget the way he swept his cousin, Kate into his strong arms, kissing her on the lips as we all watched and laughed at the "kissing cousins." I remember thinking, "Here's a man who is not afraid to show affection. A man who gathers you into his circle." Then he caught me in those arms and kissed me. My mind sent my arms up against his chest to stop the embrace, but my heart rejoiced in the attention. Yes, life would be good on this day.

JULY, 1980. The month I first made love to Don--one year after we met. He'd chosen a beautiful cottage on the Green Bay's shore. It was a full evening out. We hit many of the nightclubs: starting at Casey's Inn, hitting the C&C, the Sister Bay Bowl, the AC Tap and Florian's and then circling back to Casey's for the nightcap. From starlight into a passionate fire. I remember how unusually quiet we became and I mentioned I was nervous. He mocked me, but I think he was nervous, too. The mocking stung and I lost something in that moment. It's like something you lose when the other kids tease you in childhood play. For me, it's the loss of trust and the knowledge that now your relationship is not--cannot be--unconditional.

I became pregnant in March of 1981, after Don and I had shared another close encounter. Call it my woman's intuition, I just knew I was pregnant the next day. Of course, I didn't admit it to anyone until April, except to my old friend, Kate. I worried constantly about my life, my future, and the baby's future. I chose to be safe. I chose not to risk anything, which is now the biggest regret of my life. Kate wouldn't let me wallow in regret. "You did what you had to do for yourself and the baby at the time."

By July things had calmed down. We were anticipating the baby. I was already loving it. December would be so wonderful. A new baby. Christmas. A family. Life would be good. Week after week, Kate would stop over with a little soft, furry friend for Jana. As the collection of stuffed animals grew, the baby's room became known as The Zoo. There was even a sign on the door that read: Welcome to My Zoo.

51

1982. One year later and Jana could swim and even speak in complete sentences. The doctor agreed this was unusual and I knew I had been blessed with a "gifted" child. It became my most important goal to make sure she was given every opportunity to develop to her full potential. I fought to stay at home with her. I was criticized by my husband, Joe and his friends. Even though I did all the book work for our business, in addition to caring for the home, yard and family, I believed I was lazy and self indulgent. Trying to fill the ever-widening emptiness of my marriage with Joe--with food. Joe and I divorced when Jana was 6.

Jana filled the emptiness, too. My daughter and I would go to the cottage offered "unconditionally" by Kate. Now my dearest friend and Jana's mentor. We would heal ourselves at the cottage. Together we would build a castle out of fallen trees at our spot at Cave Point. Returning every year to see if it had survived another winter, it warmed my heart to relive those castle-building memories. Life was good.

1993. It was the last vacation with Mom. We laughed as we anticipated our evening at the Murder Mystery Theater at Maxwellton Braes. My sisters had come to Kate's cottage, too. We had cocktails on the deck as we listened to Mom tell her stories of how she had moved from Ellison Bay to California as an innocent girl of 20; met and married my father, an Air Force pilot, and at the age of 24 she had been "dragged back to God's country, on the shores of Green Bay." My sisters would roll their eyes when they heard the story once again. But now, each of us would give anything to hear them from mother's lips. Life was good.

In January Mom went to California to visit her old

friends. When she returned she mentioned she wasn't feeling well. In fact, leg pain had made sightseeing unbearable. Even shopping was a nightmare, and that woman loved to shop! Her complaints fell on unsympathetic ears out West. She lost something with that old friend and did not have the luxury of enough time to make it whole again.

Jana was on a student exchange trip to Russia when her grandmother died and had not really mourned her death. I spent over a thousand dollars trying to cover her pain--make her happy. But I was really trying to make myself happy. I needed something for myself. So, I bought my first home.

It was the first month I lived in my very own home. Not a house, but my own home. Eleven years of living in an apartment had made the prospects of decorating my own home exhilarating. It gave me great pleasure just to be able to hang a picture wherever I wanted. Home to me, means comfort.

From my journal . . . *Today, I've made some wonderful home improvements. The compact dining room seems larger because it looks out onto the cedar deck that is canopied by a huge, old maple. The new curtains open the room up even more. My spacious backyard frames the majestic pines and my many individual gardens. The gardens have become my sanctuary. I spend hours moving the plants and shrubs around. I purchased most of them at Sunny Point Gardens. Roses explode in this zone. Jana decided on a red, white and purple theme this year. She's a real gardener. I'm the designer and main-tenance person. A true labor of love and it's some-thing else we can share.*

53

I converted my living room into a cozy room where I can curl up with old and new books. I recently reread Bridges of Madison County. *And rewrote my own ending to it. Other rooms are filled with photos of family and close friends. My high school graduation photo is framed and mounted next to Jana's. Kate and I roared when we hung them. Flashback to 1966. We discovered Kate and I shared the same hairdo. One large wall was reserved for the "gifted" child's accomplishments. Medals, awards and other certificates of achievements proudly displayed for all the visitors to see and for Mother Superior to admire. Life is definitely good knowing my child is such a gem!*

This was not the month my older sister, Saddie, died. She died in August when her heart suddenly stopped beating. It was the end of summer. The end of a long friendship and so much love. I thank God I still have July to look forward to.

1998. This is the first year I've spent my vacation alone. Still, I looked forward to each day. I told myself, "I'm going to do what I want to do." I hunted for antiques; shopped for new clothes; swam at the beach-- absorbed the rays of the sun. Started to feel like my old self and recover from the losses of the last few years.

JULY is my month of hope. Life can be good in July, or December or any month as long as there is hope in your heart. I think God gave me a never-ending supply of it. He gave me good friends like Kate to help me remember all the good things of the past and focus on the promise of the summers yet to be.

GAIL ANDERSON

August - Climbing Kilimanjaro
Notes From The First Time
by
Gloria Zager

A brunette, five feet four inches tall with green eyes, Gail Anderson continues to travel to exotic locations to study birds and wildlife. Her husband, Jim, told her long ago, "Just go. Nothing will happen to you." So she travels around the world, many times without him, on EarthView expeditions--especially if it has anything to do with birding.

Preparing to host the Literary Guild meeting Gail thought to herself, *I want to fix my Peanut Butter & Squash Soup recipe. Can't resist going back to my travel journal and reading the first time I climbed the mountain--and survived.*

<u>1978. February 12:</u> England. I'm forced to resort to wool socks in bed. Wished Jimmy were here to warm my feet. This morning I found the hot water bottle behind the bathroom door. Went to Windsor Castle. Very ornate. Touristy. Plane to Kilimanjaro late.

Left at 7:00 p.m. Plane stopped at Khartoum, Sudan and proceeded to Arusha. Total 10 hours--all night. Plane packed. Uncomfortable. Finally Africa.

Surprised to find it is very lush and green with red flame plants along the road. We stopped at Hotel Tarangire for a Pilsner beer. Very nice hotel. On to Hotel Meru beneath Mt. Meru which I thought very majestic and mistook for Kilimanjaro.

On the plane over I read Hemingway's *The Snows of Kilimanjaro* again. I've made the purpose of my trip the same as the character in the novel. *I need to work the fat off my soul.*

I've spent many pleasant moments thinking of this day. If only I can get to the top. At dinner tonight, boiled ox tongue, and plenty of conversation.

> "... *a good case for New York*
> *declaring immediate bankruptcy*
> *for getting labor agreements*
> *previously made into court and*
> *starting over ... and how California*
> *wants to take water from the*
> *Columbus River in Washington ...*
> *and how Fred, the baby doctor,*
> *shoots storks as his competitors."*

Tim and Fred came up with a discussion on basic research which I found, even though much of it has no relevance, appealing to me much more than work involving journalism. My conceit telling me that I was doing something extraordinary here. Not so. It is a tourist area and I will have to draw on the undertones from it; meaning the feeling of originally comprehending

56

Kilimanjaro.

I did not pass the health requirements to get into Tanzania. I lacked a cholera shot. I was hustled into a back room and given one. I am reacting to it somewhat. I'm anxious about the dirty needle possibility. Tomorrow is a tented safari to Tarangire Park.

Fred teaches us more about Africa. a) Talk of mastiffs, his favorite dog. Known for guard and herd dogs. b) Cheetahs run 80 miles per hour, but only for short distances; 200 yards. But can run all day at 40 mph. Lose most of their catches to hyenas and lions. Tough life.

A guy came through customs with a hang glider to do Kilimanjaro. The highest peak in the world that has been glided is in Peru. He glided from 22,300 feet in the air for 35 minutes.

February 13: Monday. It is 4:00 a.m. Sandy's birthday. Never went back to sleep. Went for a walk, 6:30 a.m. to watch the sun rise. Two pictures from hotel; one of a conglomeration of bird nests, Weavers-- little yellow birds--fifty singing in one tree; the other picture of Mt. Meru.

To Tarangire Park. I cannot believe where I am. Sitting before my own tent looking past a huge tree down into a valley where a herd of elephant are washing themselves and giraffes are forming a single line up from the river which winds through the valley. Today we have seen many ostrich, elephants, giraffe, hedge hogs, egrets and many deer-types that I do not know. Fred admonished us for calling "antelope", deer.

Just finished a lovely meal of goulash with British-type tea on the veranda. Now in the shade of my tent, a

57

gentle breeze drifts over me. A little lizard passes my chair. I am content. We will wait until sundown to go out again. At least I've seen giraffes and elephants . . . and wart hogs (not hedge hogs!).

February 14: It seems like yesterday was a dream. The same as it will when I get back home. I fell asleep early, I think mostly due to lack of sleep the night before. We had some Pilsner which I am drinking to maintain most of my fluid intake. Then a good dinner of roast beef and coffee, before a bonfire. To bed at 9:30 p.m.

February 15: Woke at 5:30 a.m. I think I also woke the whole world, peeing in my bucket. I must go now and watch the sunrise again. This morning I saw my first lion and rhino. Great sight. "Many more lions are about, but the grass is too high to see them," says Zubuli, our guide. I still think the giraffes are my favorite. I slept this afternoon for it is unbearably hot.

My health is good, although I have a canker on my tongue and sore throat is beginning, so I started taking penicillin to nip it. It is too early in this trip to start this business.

There are a few raindrops hitting my thatched-roof-- quiet sounds. The evenings are pleasantly cool, but cool enough for blankets. The days are plenty hot with the biting tetse flies and they are thick by noon. The savannah seems to be in bloom for there is a lot of sneezing going on. Jimmy seems very close, although he is half a world away. I am again content except for my insatiable appetite which cannot be abated. I walked this morning at dawn to the airport and Alex passed me four times; jogging. He will be the star besides Tim who falls in love with every knoll he sees.

This morning we saw our first lioness. She was unconcerned as could be with us. Plotting slowly and steadily through the grass, resting on a termite hill and a shade tree, she was stalking a wart hog. We saw a thick grouping of impala, a dicdic, water buck and hardy beasts and a herd of elephants. I'd estimate 400-- trumpeting and carrying on.

February 16: This morning I was accompanied by a blacksmith plover who makes a noise like two pieces of metal clacking together, hence his name. One member has a case of *tourista*, which I assume is diarrhea. We are drinking the water. As of today, I am still well.

Saw clip-springers, little antelope that hop from rock to rock. And a tree hyrax, a rodent-like animal, but not a rodent. It is related to the elephant.

February 17: We left for Tarangire. Getting out on the Serengeti plains (not in our itinerary) to Ndutu Lodge. A little oasis with a lake in the middle of the hot, dry Serengeti. Saw many tommies (gazelles) and grant gazelles--thousands of them. And hundreds of wildebeest. Many zebra, giraffe.

It is these times of great migrations, I feel exhilarated. Got pictures of jackals, bustards (bird), stork, etc. The lodges are literally empty because of the Kenya-Tanzania border dispute. We heard that it was instigated by Tanzania to keep Nairobi from collecting all the money by chartering out of Nairobi into Tanzanian Parks. Also saw beautiful chestnut-colored topi. Was astounded by the mirages which were everywhere. I can't remember having seen one before. It appeared little tommies were standing in water.

February 18: Now I am at Ngorongoro Wildlife Lodge. Very plush. Have a terrific headache which I have been fighting all day. Am gaining an incredible amount of weight for the food is good--and getting no exercise. I guess we are at about 7500 feet and will descend into the crater and stay all day with a box lunch. Also extra. Not on the original plan. Ngorongoro was great! No tourists. In the crater, only us and one other vehicle. Thousands of animals: wildebeest, gazelle, zebra--no giraffe. Saw two lions, two lioness and three cubs. Fantastic.

We, Tim and I, sat on top of the wagon. It was great riding across the plains with wind blowing in my face. Got sun-burned. We got within 10 feet of a lioness who charged our truck. I thought she was going to fly up on top with me. I made tracks to get through the sun roof.

We got a rhino to charge the truck, too. The guides back up to the rhino. If rhinos keep coming and catch the truck, they have been known to overturn vehicles. My hands shake so badly I can't get a picture of a charging lioness or rhino. We saw a lone lioness on the savannah. As she passed, all the grazing animals turned to face her and quit eating. It was neat to see. Watching the animals who were so intent on her; they even followed her a while to see where she was going. We ate lunch in a glade with hippos; barking and splashing in their water hole. There were many egrets and we entertained ourselves with feeding our lunch to the African kites. They would catch the food in the air or grab it from your hands unexpectedly.

February 19: We were hot and tired when we left for Lake Manyara and tree-climbing lions. The hotel is large and gorgeous, overlooking the lake from the rift. On our descent to the lake we saw baboons, elephant, cape buffalo, thousands of flamingos, as in Ngorongoro. We stopped at a hot spring and finally came upon two lioness in an acacia tree. A good day. Now we are back at Mt. Meru and tomorrow will proceed to Kilimanjaro. The day in the hot sun has been tiring, yet I have a feeling the worst is yet to come.

We stopped at a native market. It is very colorful. You have to haggle (which I hate). I haggled and still ended up paying too much. We swam for a bit at the hotel and I found I have no wind left in me. My one ankle is weak and I twist it wrong every chance I get. Back to Mt. Meru Hotel. We walked downtown to Arusha to do some shopping. I bought a batik cloth. It was very expensive, but so pretty. Done by one of the better artists of batik (or so they say). I must find out how to do this.

February 20: On to Kilimanjaro. Stayed at Marangu Hotel one night. The hotel is run by an Irish woman, Mrs. Bennett, who is very thorough about getting porters together. Zabeli drove us to the gate. Started to walk at 11:00 a.m. Walked through deep forest. Hit rain about halfway. My $2.95 army poncho is very effective, but my boots got wet anyway. Arrived at Mandara hut at 2:00 p.m. Huts are all little A-frames divided in half. There are four people in each cabin. I bunk with Ed and Carly. The main dining hall had a fire. I was wet and cold and the porters didn't arrive with the bags of dry clothes until 4 more hours had passed. My boots dried somewhat. The supper was good. We ate by kerosene lanterns. After which Ed broke out the 150 proof rum for the tea. I am abstaining until I get to the top. This first day was not so bad. Tim gave us some pointers on how to walk very slowly. We, of course, didn't make it through the night without having to go to the can-- literally, squat toilets. These toilets are not a bad idea, but they stink horribly, and rarely does anyone hit the hole. One is bound to get a foot full of shit. We wait until dark and pee outside the cabin.

February 21: We woke up to rain today. Hiked all day in the downpour. Left the forest and entered the heath. Although there are many beautiful flowers, one does not see them because the climb is so hard. You focus on expending the least amount of energy. One's world becomes deciding where to put your foot next. I will look at the view on my way down. We started at 8:00 a.m. and had a 15-minute lunch, arriving at Morombo Hotel at 2:00 p.m. For the first four hours, and every rise I kept looking for the hut.

We've had our tea and are bunking down for a rest. Ed and Carly are already asleep. My health was declining from bad headaches--too much sun. However, I feel better at 9,500 feet which is Mandara. The exercise is what helped I guess. I do feel much better.

Now at Morombo, 12,200 feet, which Tim says is the critical altitude for air problems, so they'll keep us here for two days. I live now in my Icelandic sweater for it is getting colder. Morombo is fogged in, so the view isn't much. I saw Mawenzi Peak a couple of times through the clouds. Very pretty. To bed at 9:00 p.m.

Ed entertains us with his harmonica. My headaches-- two aspirins and a Dramamine later--are subsiding and I felt better this morning. A lot of coughing going on. Some worse than others. We will stay here one more day.

We need to acclimate.

February 22: The sunrise was beautiful. Now clouds are all around and below us. Most of the group will continue on and I feel like I've been left behind. But I know we have to acclimate. A few people are stopping here and will not complete the climb. One German boy--an otherwise healthy young fellow--is green. He is sitting alone on a rock and is feeling sorry for himself. A mousy-looking chipmunk is running about the hut and I'm guarding my shoes which I am still trying to dry out. Not easy at 12,000 feet. Yesterday, I put my socks by the stove pipe and it got too hot and burned up two of them. We will hike for two hours, up to 14,000 feet and back down. Alex and I took pictures of one another next to some groundsel that look like palm trees. It was just before the rain with the fog sneaking in between the trees. We were drenched, but still had a good time.

February 23: Rose at 6:15 a.m. Glorious sunrise. On road by 7:30 to Kibo hut at 15,500 feet. The lack of air is taking its toll. Five and a half hours later, we are at Kibo. There is no wood and it is quite cold. I slept from 3:30 to 5:00. Had a supper of porridge. We will have more porridge at 1:00 a.m. when we begin our assent. A few people are making it to Gilman's Point or the summit. One group took 12 hours total and could hardly walk at Kibo. Yet, they still had 3 hours to Mocombe. The saddle between Mawenzi and Gilman's Peak proved to be very slow going. It is completely barren--which appeals to me. Carly is vomiting from the change in altitude. I took a Dramamine right away and feel fine. Almost everyone is asleep now. It is 6:30 p.m.

Other interesting notes: our sleeping bags are full of lice and we are all bit to hell.

February 24: Today we powdered our bags to slow the lice up. Spoke too soon. Woke up at 11:00 p.m. sicker than hell. Am not vomiting, but increasingly more nauseous. Dramamine doesn't help now.

February 25: Jockem wakes us at 1:00 a.m. for more porridge. I cannot even look at it. It is cold, maybe about 20 degrees. Carly is still sick, too. We suit up. The moon is full when we set out for the steepest, hardest part of our trip. My body has no energy at all. Carly is in front of me and she is gagging. This does not help my stomach in any way. I know she wants to go back, but Tim says, " Only a little farther, try it." We've walked for 6 hours--at least a 20 degree grade--with no air and increasing altitude sickness. Now almost everyone has the headache, except Fred.

February 26: The sun rose over Mawenzi around 7:00 a.m. Incredibly beautiful. I did not get a picture of it. One of the guides was carrying my knapsack with my camera and I was too sick to pull it out. We reached the top by 8:00 a.m. and looked into the crater of Kilimanjaro with its strange, melting glacier that drops vertically. Most don't melt that way. I went up to sign the book at Gilman's Peak. Took a couple of pictures in which I tried to smile. Fred fell immediately to sleep in the intense sunlight. We don't stay long becauseTim says we will only get sicker. It takes 2 1/2 hours to run down the hill, stopping every few minutes to gag. We stop once, so Fred can put on his skiis which were toted all the way up the mountain. At last, he can declare he was the Kilimanjaro Ski Club. Upon returning to Kibo, I immediately hit the sack and skipped dinner. My legs are wobbly and I feel better after taking an aspirin for my headache. Tim has given me two compozine to settle my stomach. But, no luck. After I woke up I was much better and we left Kibo at 2:00 p.m. Seven more miles, but all down hill. Ed started out early as he is developing tendinitis. Fred's knees are about shot. I feel wonderful! The euphoria is setting in from all the adrenalin that pumped in from the stress of climbing this peak. I stayed back with Tim and Fred. Tim and I would walk ahead and sit and wait for Fred.

I think this is the most beautful part of the trip. The clouds roll across the saddle and envelope us with no rain. It is eerie and beautiful. I just can't believe that I have climbed Kilimanjaro!

It takes Fred until 6:30 to get down. I've finally left Tim because I just want to be alone and rejoice. Think about home and Jimmy.

February 27: Fred cannot walk any farther and we have 14 miles to go today. The porters will have to take him down in an aqua, which is a stretcher with wheels under it. It is guided by five porters. Ed is not much better, but is hobbling along. Last night Fred and Alex talked of drilling through Ed's big toenails to relieve the pressure of the blood pooled there. His long nails were torn up as he walked down the mountain.

I am free to go slow and take pictures. What a beautiful day it is. We took an alternative route back down, through the jungle. Alex, Carly and I stopped once in a pretty glade to watch some beautiful butterflies glide about. We are at our hotel by 4:00 p.m. Pretty stiff after the 14 mile descent. Received certificates commemorating our climb. I am now dying for a bath.

February 28: I am leaving Africa. Pasting some postage stamps in my travel journal--small souvenirs of art. My feelings are so mixed. Thinking of home . . . tonight is the night that the Guild meets and I really miss Jimmy. I want to be home again, but am so sad to leave this beautiful country. Though long and hard, this trip has exceeded my expectations. Good-bye Africa.

JERRALYN SAUNDERS

September - Lakeside Resolutions
by
Steve Raap

6:02 a.m. A reluctant sun clung to the backside of the wet horizon, refusing to rise, grasping on to one last shred of darkness like a man condemned to die at dawn. The lake's whitecaps, forming and disappearing at the whim of the wind, reflected the hesitant hues of the coming morning. Scattered clouds, heavy with moisture, raced across the sky--unsure of their direction and unwilling to discard their cargo. On the beach, Lake Michigan gulls seeking protection from the impending storm, huddled together in silence.

Jerralyn Saunders, the diva of Door County, thought to herself, *If I'm the only one to witness this sunrise, at least it has an appreciative audience.* Watching from her multi-windowed, lakeside home, she savored another sip of the hazelnut coffee she had purchased from the Door County Coffee and Tea Company in Carlsville the day before.

Jerralyn preferred shopping for groceries at the Main

Street Market in Egg Harbor. To save time today, she would run into Sturgeon Bay for the special ingredients for the recipe she would serve to her "booky" guests tonight.

As she set the coffee cup down on her plant table, she said out loud, "Get at it, girl." And with that, she lowered her naked frame down on her hands and knees, assuming the cat stance so favored by the Bad-back Brigade. With a motion that seemed to match the waves outside, Jerralyn repeatedly arched her back and then relaxed her backbone. The first rays of sunlight broke the horizon's edge and their reflections began to skip and dance along the beads of perspiration that were forming along her upper lip.

Five minutes into her morning ritual, at the peak of an arching movement, Jerralyn felt a touch of fur brush and rise up against her breasts. "Good morning, Jabba," she said greeting her sofa-sized, orange tabby cat. "Please forgive me, I know I'm stealing your exercises." Jabba just plopped himself down in front of her and assumed his own position. The same position that had originally caught Jerralyn's eye when she found him living paw-to-mouth in the Door County Animal Shelter in 1991. The same position that instantly brought to mind the star-crossed, cinematic villain for whom he was named.

Jabba waited for Jerralyn's stretching regime to conclude. Bored with the whole exercise routine, the only ritual he was interested in started with the sound of a can opener and ended with a nap.

6:36 a.m. Having finished her hundred crunches and satisfying Jabba's hunger pangs with his usual dosage of cat food, Jerralyn headed for the shower. She was enjoying the rhythmic pulses of the massaging shower head against her ebony skin when the telephone rang. Quickly, she shut off the water, grabbed a towel and in a half-hearted attempt to dry herself, she entered the bedroom and answered the phone.

"Hello-o," Jerralyn chimed, as she simultaneously worked her two-foot-long dreadlocks into her yellow towel.

"Hey there, Jerri, how ya doin'?" asked the voice on the phone.

"Oh, hi Emmi. I'm just getting rolling this morning. What can I do for you?" Jerralyn wrapped the corners of her towel around and tucked them in.

"I just didn't sleep well. I've been up for hours reading that damn frog book you gave me. The storm front that moved in last night kept me up. I knew it was coming, I could feel it in my knees," Emmi complained.

"You're still coming tonight, aren't you?" Jerralyn queried, trying to get a head count for pizzas.

"Of course, especially when you're doing the cooking. What are you cooking up for us? Any hints?"

"Do you have a sombrero?" Jerralyn teased.

"Alright, Mexican! I love Mexican," Emmi exclaimed.

"Did I say Mexican? I meant to ask you if you drive an Alfa Romeo."

" Hey, wait a minute," Emmi said curiously, "Let's see, Italian car . . . Hmmm, olive oil? Pesto? Red wine? Am I getting warm?"

"I don't know if you're getting warm, but hot sauce might help," Jerralyn continued to tease her.

"Hot sauce? What are you talking about now...Cajun?" Emmi asked, attempting one more answer.

"Just bring yourself and your appetite." Jerralyn

added, "Can you come around five to help me set up?"

"Sure. Me, my appetite and my curiosity will be there. Bye for now," Emmi said, signing off.

"See you later." Jerralyn realized some excitement at being able to host the monthly meeting. Some meetings had been formal, and some of the books chosen for review were less than stimulating. The classics, self-help-- or God forbid, travel guides--bored her to death.

But, I'm not a snob, she thought. *Well-traveled? Yes.* You don't become a world-renowned opera star without putting some foreign continents under your feet. Still, she could appreciate all different kinds of people. Growing up on the south side of Chicago, she knew what it meant to be poor . . . and the value of simple living.

Jerralyn's father had given her an appreciation for the simplistic joys to be found on the shores of Lake Michigan. They shared many trips together to view the big stone museums in downtown Chicago, where she would climb upon the huge statues that guarded their entrances. She had played on most of the beaches there, too.

In fact, it was her love of Lake Michigan beaches that had brought her to Door County to live. Rather than an apartment in New York, London or Rome, she chose the area near the Whitefish Bay dunes. Yes, it was inconvenient at times to fly out of Green Bay or Milwaukee to performances around the world. But it was a small price to pay for living on the water's edge in Door. The water, over time, had become her lifeblood.

No, she was not a *snob*. It's just that she'd rather hear a review of something delicious, like a great cookbook, rather than another book on travel ! Tonight, it was her turn to host the group and hopefully offer a new perspective on life. And it wouldn't be because she was the only black woman in the club. No, the book she had chosen had little to do with being black in Door County. If anything, it had more to do with the staples of Door County living: money, power and sex.

That's why Jerralyn bought each member a copy of Tom Robbin's novel, *Half Asleep in Frog Pajamas*. If that book didn't get their individual juices flowing, no book could!

10:47 a.m. Jerralyn kissed Jabba on her way out the door. "Be good, my little Hut Muppet," she whispered in Jabba's fuzzy ear. He responded typically for an overlord, with a half-baked sneer that turned into a full-fledged yawn. "Oh, so sorry to wake you, your highness," Jerralyn laughed as she pulled the door closed.

She descended the treated-lumber staircase and walked briskly up the loose stone driveway to her garage. On the way, she activated her remote-controlled door opener, which revealed her pride and joy: a turquoise '98 Boxster convertible. She had little guilt or conflict with living simply and owning this flashy European set of wheels. Guilt had long since been blown away by the warm, peninsula winds that whipped her Rastafarian mane in all directions as she crisscrossed over two state highways and dozens of county roads, heading from her Lake Michigan shore toward the waters of Green Bay.

"If I have to drive to TitleTown to meet my planes, I might as well enjoy the ride," she had told her father on one of his infrequent visits north. He agreed.

"I don't begrudge anyone a comfortable ride," he had said. "After all, that was my business."

Jerralyn's father, James Sauders, had spent his adult life in transportation. He served a mostly white customer base as a porter on the Great Northern train line that ran between Chicago and Seattle. His weekly trips out to the West Coast and back for the better part of forty years kept his family fatherless, but fed. During his weekends he'd devote all his time to Jerralyn and his wife, Benita.

James Saunders' pride in his family was reflected in the service he'd provide on board his assigned coaches of the train. He'd see to every need with a smile and a tip of his porter's cap. He was glad to be working, especially after all the World War II veterans, of which he was one, came home looking for work.

He enjoyed making other people feel comfortable for the 37-hour trip. Officially, he was on duty for the entire ride. Yet, he never complained--even when a passenger would wake him at 2:00 a.m. for some bizarre request.

The fruits of his labor were born in the achievements of his daughter. Having a natural talent at a young age, Jerralyn became the inspiration that led James to provide a measure of exemplary service. That in turn would provide excellent tips. Those tips meant money enough for Jerralyn to begin singing lessons at the age of seven.

Jerralyn couldn't help but think of her father each time she turned on the ignition of her new car. She knew he had sacrificed a lot to make this all happen. And she would always be grateful. Yet, when Jerralyn's mother passed away in her sleep, just two years ago, James declined her invitation to move in with her. "I just want to stay in my own home and enjoy the memories," he had told her. "You've got your own life, traveling around the world and all. You don't need to be worrying about me livin' at your place. I've got good neighbors and my museums to take care of me. I'll be fine. You just sing your heart out and we'll call it even."

So, even it is, Jerralyn thought. She pointed, "Boxy" down Cave Point Drive and headed toward Sturgeon Bay.

10:59 a.m. As she turned off onto Highway 42 just south of Highway 57, she couldn't resist looking at the remains of the Starlight Drive-In Theater sign on her left. "Why can't somebody take that damn eye sore down!" she mumbled to herself. She had hated that sign since the day she moved to Door. How many years had the drive-in been closed? Twenty? Where was the community pride? Who was responsible for civic improvements? She thought, *No one, I guess.*

So, for the past twenty years, every time she passed the rusted sign she made a conscious effort *not* to look at it. And during those hundreds of trips into or around Sturgeon Bay, her eyes were drawn to it every time.

This time Jerrayln pulled over to the shoulder of the highway. She stopped the car across from the hulky, tilted sign that was ever-so-slowly sinking into the soft earth. She stared out her driver side window, studying the sign for the first time, as if peering at mangled bodies in an auto accident. Her heart beat quickened. And she knew why.

She didn't need a shrink's psycho-babble to explain it to her at all. She had long ago figured out the connection between the sign and the worst day of her 44-year-old life.

Now the horrible images were once again flooding back into her consciousness like a scratchy, foreign, black-and-white film that had been spliced too many times, sprocket holes missing . . . 5 . . . 4 . . . 3 . . . 2 . . .

FADE IN: South Chicago drive-in theater.
OPENING SHOT: "Very much like the Starlight,"
Freud might say . . .
CUT TO: The college senior, whose name you
dare not to remember.
PAN TO: His nasty beater of a car.
CUT TO: His heavy body, pinning you down.
INTER CUT: Your cries for help--
begging him to stop.
ZOOM IN: A two-shot as his sweat drips down into
your tear-filled eyes.
MUSIC SWELLS: The groan of his release
crescendos with your cries of pain.
DOLLY BACK: During his silence--your silence.
CROSS FADE: The long drive home.
CUT TO: A long shot in the spotlight of
your fear--afraid to tell.
FADE TO BLACK: Your memory submersion.
END TITLE: Finis.

The horror of those images had remained with Jerralyn for over twenty years. Yet, sitting in her car on that busy curve, she came to a new realization. Like the Starlight sign before her, she too had survived. Unlike the sign's extinguished beacon, she had actually thrived in the years since. She always felt that if she had survived that awful night, she could do damn near anything. And she had.

In fact, as far as she was concerned, she thought now she might have gotten to the point where she was starting to grow fond of that old rust magnet. Suddenly, she noticed that the dull red paint wasn't just fading into pink, it was starting to peel off the metal beneath it.

That might not be good, she thought. Then she realized her drastic turn around and was shocked by her change in attitude. What, for years, had been a sub-liminal reminder of her most wretched pain, now became a symbol of her most glorious triumph. From hell-bent destruction to proud preservation.

She laughed out loud. A long, deep, heartfelt laugh of resolution. Jerralyn thought, *This old sign may outlast me.* She gave the sign a Girl Scout salute, checked her rearview mirror and turned "Boxy" back onto the highway. She didn't look back.

12:09 p.m. Having taken her time in selecting the most succulent, freshest tomatoes, onions and green peppers available, Jerralyn loaded all the groceries into her car and headed for home. As she passed the Starlight sign once again, she honked her horn--twice. Finally she had made peace with the past.

12:28 p.m. Jerralyn turned her car into her driveway, stopping at the road's edge to check her mail. *Bills, bills, sweepstakes, bills, magazines. Boring! Doesn't anyone write letters anymore?* Then she proceeded down past the bend in her driveway and noticed a red Volkswagen Beetle parked by the house.

"Dad!" she exclaimed. The red 1979 VW could only be his. No one that she knew would even consider driving one . . . especially one that old. Yet, his car looked as clean and bright as the day he bought it.

She remembered that day. Nineteen years ago she had returned from shopping when her dad drove into her driveway behind the wheel of this red bug. "Had to buy it, honey," he had said. "After this year, they won't be

75

makin' 'em anymore. Gotta take good care of this one, so it'll last."

And last it had. Jerralyn thought about all the Volkswagens her father had owned. She also remembered the kidding she took from her friends in the neighborhood. Back then, it just wasn't cool for a black man to be driving a VW.

"Look, child," he had said, "If we can save some money on payments and gas, then that means you might really be able to go to a fancy singin' school. Doesn't that make sense?"

It did. After that, Jerralyn gladly took the ribbing from her friends. She had bigger dreams to realize.

Now, here it was, one of the last VW's, glistening in the rain. But where was her father? She called out again. "Dad?" No answer. She two-stepped up the stairway to her front door and turned the knob. It was still locked. She inserted the key and opened the door. With long strides she went over to the sliding glass doors that faced the lake. Through the glass Jerralyn could see him standing alone down on the beach, hands in his pockets, facing the water.

She slid one of the doors open and called out to James. There was no reaction. *Can't hear me above the sound of the waves.* She crossed the deck; stepped down onto the wet sand. Within minutes she slid in behind her father, encircled his waist with her arms and gave him a big hug. Somehow he seemed skinnier than she had remembered.

"Hey, Pop," Jerralyn spoke softly into his ear. "I've missed you."

"I've missed you too, Kitten," James replied. He turned around and gave his daughter the once over. "Are you sure you're eating enough? You look a bit thin to me."

"Me?" she answered, "What about you, Pop? You're not living on ice cream and popcorn again, are you?"

"Nah, I'm O.K. Just kinda tired these days."

Jerralyn grabbed James' hand and the two started walking back to the house.

"To what do I owe this visit?" she asked him directly.

"Hey, can't a father pop in on his daughter without playing twenty questions?" James replied. It was a tone that told Jerralyn something was not quite right.

Concerned, she told him, "I'm only asking because you usually call me to tell me you're coming. 'Fair warning' you used to tell me."

"Yeah, I know," and then he added, "I'm sorry, Kitten. I've just got some news that isn't too good. I didn't really know how to tell you . . . or even if I should."

"What is it, Dad? What's wrong?" Jerralyn asked, concern evident in her voice.

"Let's get inside where it's warmer. I'm getting too chilled out here."

The two made their way up the steps of the deck and into the house. Jerralyn pulled out a quilt for James to wrap himself in, and microwaved some milk, while preparing two cups of hot chocolate.

"Hot chocolate, coming up!" Jerralyn announced cheerily, trying to disguise her anxiety. James didn't say anything. He was staring at the floor, deep in his own thoughts.

Jerralyn served the hot chocolate. Her dad sat with his feet up on the sofa. Jabba had already made his presence known by plopping himself down by James' feet.

"The cat rules this roost, eh?" James asked, "Makes a damn fine foot warmer."

"He sure does," Jerralyn agreed, "Jabba enjoys your visits as much as I do."

She could tell James was searching for the right words. He tried to go on, "I appreciate your hospitality . . . your cat . . . everything about you. I . . . "

"Oh Pop, what is it?" Jerralyn cried out. "Tell me what's wrong." She leapt off her chair and knelt down beside her father, holding his hands. Tears welled-up in her eyes, then spilled over onto her cheeks.

"Well, Kitten, it's just . . . just that . . . I'm . . . I've got . . . Oh, hell. I wish I didn't have to tell you, but . . . "

"But what, Dad? Please tell me," she pleaded.

"I've got . . . I've got . . . cancer. There, I said it. I've told you."

"Oh, Dad!" Jerralyn cried, sobbing uncontrollably.

"The doctors confirmed it. They told me I've got anywhere from six weeks to three months."

Jerralyn buried her face in James' chest while he tried to comfort her. "There, there Kitten. It's O.K. It really is. To tell you the truth, I'm kinda lookin' forward to seeing your mother again."

Jerralyn's sobbing gradually subsided. She lifted her head and gazed into her father's eyes, the same, sparkling hazel eyes she had loved her whole life. "Isn't there anything we can do, Dad?" Then she added, "What kind of cancer is it?"

"Colon, honey," James replied. "Probably too much train food and not enough of your mother's good cookin'. But what can I say? We've got some time left. Time to enjoy each other. That is, if your invite is still good."

"Oh Dad, you know it is. But what about all of your things?"

"Oh, I've brought everything I'll need in my car. The big stuff, furniture and all, I put into storage. You can sort through that stuff later. Sell what you don't want to keep. I got rid of the apartment already. So, there's really not much to worry about--except me and you and how we're going to enjoy each other."

"For as long as we can. But how long have you known?"

"Six months."

"Six months! Why didn't you tell me sooner?"

"It took me a while to absorb it all. And what good would it have done? I wanted to make sure, before I told you. It gave me time to go through things, old memory boxes, photographs, you know . . . stuff that you don't even remember."

"It wouldn't have been a worry, Dad," Jerralyn said. "But I appreciate it just the same. You're always looking out for me." She gave James a big, long hug and then kissed his cheek. She got up, finished off her lukewarm chocolate, and stood awkwardly, trying to figure out what to do first. "I think it's about time *I* started doing for *YOU*, Dad! Are you alright? Is there anything I can get you?"

"No, not really," James assured her. "I just want to be part of your days, that's all. What're you doin' the rest of the day?"

"Oh, God! I've still got groceries in the car and eleven people showing up in less than five hours for dinner and a book club meeting. But, hey, maybe I can call them and cancel the . . . "

"Don't you do it, girl," James warmly added, "I'd love to meet your friends up here. What's the name of the book you all are reading?"

"It's that Tom Robbins' novel you gave me last year."

"*Frog Pajamas?* Oh, I loved that book. What a writer that guy is . . . and the descriptions! Can you believe some of those ramblings? Absolutely incredible!"

"Yeah, he is wonderful," Jerralyn agreed. "I'm sure glad you turned me on to him."

"Me, too. Why don't we get those groceries up from the car? I can help you get dinner started. What are we makin'?"

"Oh, Gourmet Pizza on the Grill," Jerralyn answered.

"My favorite!"

"Are you sure you're O.K.? . . . to do this tonight? I could call . . . "

James reassured her again, "I said it's Okay. Let's stop yappin' and get things ready."

5:12 p.m. While her father took a nap in the downstairs guest room, Jerralyn opened a Door brew. She had cut a slice of lime, thinking, *Oh, how this day has changed everything.* She squeezed the lime into the beer. It drifted slowly toward the bottom of the brown glass bottle.

It's been one hell of a day, but Pop seems to be handling all this so well, she thought to herself. *I only hope I can be as strong when he really needs me. Lord knows, that won't be too far off.*

Jerralyn turned to look out her kitchen window. Glancing past the red VW, she noticed the first one arriving for the meeting. It was Emmi. *Thank God for good friends,* Jerralyn thought.

80

EMMI JOHNSTON

October Reflections
by
DyAnne Korda

Emmi Johnston is religious about keeping a journal. Not daily entries, but an on-going record of thoughts about her life. She incorporates them into performance pieces as well as handmade chapbooks, filled with her poetry and artworks.

<u>October 1:</u> There is a power in our circle. In this honesty, in speaking our minds and in listening to one another.

I'm looking forward to hosting Door County's oldest club this month. When we gather together, there are no barriers and no airs. We welcome one another into our homes. We see, feel, and learn what each one cherishes-- a certain passage of words on the page; a grandchild cutting her first tooth; or a thriving garden filled with blue phlox, bleeding hearts, and purple cone flowers.

However philosophies differ surrounding each book, we hear each other out. What did Joy Harjo really mean in her poem, "She Had Some Horses?" How much of Larry Watson's *Montana 1948* is fiction? *I liked Justice better.*

It angers me that women's opinions, intuition and wisdom have been held down for thousands of years by Everyman who ruled Everything. Once I heard Ram Dass say on Wisconsin Public Radio that the American culture values knowledge, not wisdom. Right on. Yet men who think with their hearts, like Dass, are around. I married one. And I believe there are more in the making. The millennium will enter with peace.

October 3: We came here to remember to breathe.

This renovated red brick farmhouse stands hidden from any blacktop road. High on a craggy bluff in Egg Harbor, our home overlooks Green Bay. We've always had a need to accompany water through the seasons. We love to feel her life-giving breath at our door year round. From the cool blueness of summer waves that swish upward toward the fierce noon sun to the secure stone-like stance of the ice on the bay.

Tom and I didn't want to build a new home. Such a waste of land and resources. So, when the old Lautenbach farm went up for sale, we were high bidders. We did, however, tear down walls to install windows wherever possible. To bring the outdoors in. The largest picture window points toward Chambers Island. We also reconstructed a gigantic screen porch to better commune with Green Bay even during the most inclement weather. To watch Mother Nature play the same as our three cats do with the autumn leaves. Wind rising. Waves rolling and pouncing.

We set benches in our yard so we can follow the sun

through the herb and wildflower gardens. Around catnip, lavender, columbine, chamomile, mint, sage and rosemary. We follow the sun around trillium, forget-me-nots, lupine, wild roses, bottle gentian and brilliant poppies. Benches grace spots where we can sit with some of our Gaia sculptures. Like the gentle Sleeping Goddess of Malta and the grand figure we call Tree Spirit Woman. We have a bench near the shed that Tom uses as his writing office. The same shed that stores our beloved Harley Davidson.

A stone fireplace marks the center of our living room. Walls are lined with book shelves, CD and cassette music racks. Our musical tastes range from Edith Piaf to Laurie Anderson. From Mozart to Clint Black. We have the paintings and pottery of friends, with much of my own pieces throughout the house. Candles, stones, branches that I collect; all rest in corners and on shelves. Our funiture is an "eclectic mix." Grandmother's chairs and coffee table, a sister's couch, a hand-me-down-television, my first rocking chair. If it's comfortable, we'll take it. The 1950's kitchen set of royal blue chairs with flamingo pink table came from Tom's great aunt.

Aromas of pinion and cedar incense blend with percolated morning coffee and float from room to room.

October 6: I transplanted wild iris and tiger lilies inside a semi-circle of four boulders left by ancient glacier movements. Drops of almost-freezing rain chinked through the leaves dangling from branches above me. With shovel in hand, I dug dirt and then broke the roots by hand. The sweet sighs of wet earth, my hair dripping, and the wind weaving around us--blessing us. These woods reassure me. Confirm that I am home.

October 8:

> *I wrap dawn's silence*
> *around me as if it were*
> *a precious wool shawl.*

To welcome the chill and morning creatures--squirrels, finches, blue jays, chickadees--I open the back door, grab cracked ice cream pails, dip them in the garbage can stuffed to the brim with black sunflower seed. I toss two or three dried corn cobs across the fallen yellow birch leaves, the red maple leaves. A blade of grass pokes through here and there. Air is thick with dampness. Birds chirp and call when they hear seeds swoosh from pail to feeder.

I'm inside the kitchen, pouring hot coffee . . . *Is my cup cracked? Is that a cat hair? Cracked* . . . and battling a napping cat for space at my desk, I bend over a worn journal with pen. Now, the outside feeders hold hungry customers at each perch.

October 9: I write this with the eldest cat slung over my shoulder and jasmine tea steaming from my clay cup.

The morning sun plays tag with shadows on tree trunks and stones outside my window. The air is crisp. Only earliest chickadees demand seed. Too early for the hordes of chipmunks who dive underneath stacked wood, scattering fallen leaves, stuffing pouches so full, they look like Dizzy Gillespie hitting a high note on his trumpet.

October 12: Yesterday's walk was a scene out of a Gabriel Garcia Marquez novel. Something like his beautiful *One Hundred Years of Solitude*. The weather, at 70 degrees, was unusually warm for October. Tom and I walked down the road and enjoyed the Indian Summer breeze. As we turned a corner and came to a clearing, clouds of lady bugs descended upon us with rounded wings like tiny parachutes. Swarms of beetles blanketed me. Tom stopped counting at 63. In my hair, every inch of my t-shirt, jeans, my battered sandals. *Lady Bugs. Whenever they have visited with me before, it has been a lovely omen that my life was about to make an exciting change. And this visit--so many!*

As we walked further, some landed on Tom, too. Deep pumpkin orange. A combination of black spots on folded wings. We continued in joy, talking about nothing in particular. A red tail hawk circled above us in the cloudless sky. Those are the animals that Tom looks toward for comfort. He was so glad to see them.

I found a nice white rock which resembles a three pound piece of pita bread and I had to scoop it up. It is a definite possibility for my "Works by Water and Wind" exhibit. It will be comprised mostly of rocks and driftwood found near and around Green Bay. Ever since I was little, I believed that rocks are beautiful sculptures made by Nature, herself.

We also noticed two white seagull feathers skimming across the road. Tom cupped them carefully in his hands since I carried the pita stone. Upon reaching our door, we thoroughly checked our clothes for the few remaining lady bugs. After we thanked them, we brushed them away.

October 15: October weekends offer afternoon symphonies of whining chain saws; Wisconsin prepares to brighten and warm the coming winter. Tom and I joined in the merriment and rhythm of chopping wood and stacking logs.

This morning we jumped in the truck and whipped down the winding road to the Dunn Family farm to buy a few cords of maple and oak. Bailey, the black lab, didn't disappoint us; as usual she greeted us at the edge of the road to race with our truck, snapping at the back tires all the way. Bunches of cats--every size, shape, and color-- literally emerged from the woodwork. Tiny orange tiger triplets circled my feet, two handsome black and white adolescent cats trotted behind us to the wood piles. They climbed in and popped out of the piles as we attempted to load the truck bed.

The whole of the afternoon and into the early evening we unloaded, chopped, and stacked wood. Afterwards we rewarded ourselves with cold beers and the best hamburgers in Door County at Mike's Port Pub in Jacksonport.

October 18: Why didn't the poet from long ago begin his verse something like, "There is nothing so rare as a day in October . . . " Maybe the rhyme scheme wouldn't be so great, but every year October delights us with the depth of her beauty. Birch, maple, oak remind us how easily they can transform their leaves into a living storybook--splashes of gold, orange, red and rust. It's an artist's dream. All this gaudy color swirls and presses against wide blue skies. Skies are always bluer in autumn and Green Bay's waves perform crazy im- provisational dances during this month. Scarlet apples taste their juiciest.

Tom and I gather with friends at Trio downtown to celebrate the harvest of autumn's gifts. A few other evenings are marked on the calendar: 1) The Cider Pressing Party on Washington Island; 2) The Pumpkin Patch Festival in Egg Harbor . . . with farmer's markets, outdoor entertainment, and what Tom and I refer to as the annual "Maybe-we'll-win-next-year-Chili Contest; and 3) Sister Bay's Fall Festival.

October 21: Frost tinted the leaves gold. Most leaves have crumbled to rust. The bay explodes with wild, white foam waves. I reluctantly put my sandals away for the weather has turned early this year. I was barefoot most of the summer. Now I pull out shoes. I start with cloth tennis shoes, then graduate to my red high-tops or clogs with heavy socks, and finally to Sorrel boots. I trade-in my t-shirts and wrap-around skirts for long johns, jeans, turtlenecks and sweaters. I fluff the afghans on the couch in anticipation of the long evening hours ahead.

October 24: To celebrate Halloween/Samhain and to decorate our home for the gathering of the Literary Guild:

In vases I've arranged collections of fallen leaves and delicate twigs. Apples, hazelnuts and pomegranates rest in a ceramic bowl near four earth-scented candles marking the four directions on our coffee table.

I've chosen favorite stones (the one shaped like a miniature white piano, the one that resembles the perfect, oval ostrich egg . . . and I've picked through my shoe box of animal bones. Now these stones and bones pose in corners and on tables with gnarled pieces of driftwood or thin tree sticks meticulously chiseled by beaver teeth.

To remember family members and friends who have

died, we've placed their photos and a few momemtos: a pocket knife, a doily, a knitting needle, sheet music . . . between two large candles on top of the fireplace. Long ago people believed that during Halloween, the veil between the worlds is thinnest.

Plastic black cats and shiny plaster skulls have been squeezed inside any open space between jam jars, house plants, phone books, CD racks, and framed photos. We've strung tiny pumpkin lights around the living room doorway, wove them around the stone fireplace and up the staircase. We've hung paper skeletons in windows and every spare hook in the house. Of course, the honored pumpkin has taken its place as the kitchen table centerpiece.

I borrowed a few straight-backed chairs for some of the older members. I'll be looking out the window so I can run outside to help them up the steps and through the front door when they arrive.

October 29: It was hard to choose a book for the Literary Guild discussion tomorrow. I wanted something to reflect October's magic--something on the order of the exotic and dream-like *Griffin and Sabine* series by Nick Bantock (which includes *Griffin and Sabine, Sabine's Notebook* and *The Golden Mean*). I love the mysterious letter writing format, the landscapes, the breathtaking artwork and the extraordinary story.

I wanted a book that was not only magical, but which also honors the intricate relationships between women. The Guild does this for me. So I picked *Dreaming in Cuban* by Cristina Garcia. Not only is the language sensual and lyrical, but this novel blends the ordinary with the supernatural exquisitely. Perfect for an autumn booklover's meeting.

Now for food and drink. Maybe a hearty pumpkin soup or a flavorful stew with all the fall vegetables that I can scrounge--carrot, turnip, potato . . . I'll serve warm, dark bread. Pumpernickel for Inge. Mulled red wine with cinnamon sticks or steaming hot apple cider. Then for dessert, "Hecate's Apple Pretty." The moist, rich, earthy cake recipe that I found in <u>A Wise Woman's Garden</u> (October 1996).

After much talk, after stomachs are full, we'll gather around the fireplace and I'll bring out the tarot cards. Since Halloween activities usually revolve around the comings and goings of spirits, this is the time to receive guidance from beyond and from deep inside ourselves.

I've seen tarot cards encourage people to speak more freely, to become childlike in voicing needs and as-pirations. Sharing insights provided by card images can enhance trust, exploration, and care through meaningful conversations. This nourishes our spirits--especially be-fore we accept winter's gift of darkness. The time for rest and peace. So, who will explore the mysteries of our own intuition? Who will celebrate this gentle inner wisdom with me?

October Reflections

INGE MUELLER

Three November Letters
by
Ilse Dietsche

November 1, 1996

Hello my friend !

It is the first of November and my thoughts go home to my old country. Do you have some time and may I come for a "paper-visit?" Get yourself a cup of coffee and listen to my news.

I moved to a remote area in Door County, a peninsula in northeastern Wisconsin. I live now in a log cabin surrounded by woods. The first floor is one big room; the kitchen separated by a hand-picked stone wall fireplace. The living room has comfortable davenports and low tables. I have lots of memorabilia hanging on the walls, including things from our former hunting days. The individual lamps make small islands for visitors, conversation and reading. The kitchen also is my dining room. Everything is roughly built in. I have a big telephone wire roll for a table. The round top fills out the corner with a beautiful view of Green Bay, especially now when the leaves are gone. Upstairs are three bedrooms; one is a computer den, where I intend to write my life story and memories I can give to my children. Just got news from my daughter who visited Germany and she told me how happy she was to find some old letters I once wrote to my parents. How she found out so much about herself in them. This art of responding and writing will be lost with all the "computer mail" and telephone conversations. Prepared a Rotary program that I can use when people ask me "to speak." I couldn't have done this idea, if it weren't for the letters the travelers once wrote long ago. I like holding them and rereading the writers' thoughts--having something in my hands that they have touched and felt. Sentimental? Yes, I am.

Let's go back to the second floor and invite you to see more of the house. One room is always open for guests. For myself I picked out the biggest room with a walk-in bathroom and a walk-out sun deck. The hallway around the steps could be used differently, but I made a cozy TV corner and top to bottom bookshelves. One wall is for all my slides and "photo stuff." As you know, I'm still traveling a lot and keep a record in words and pictures.

So, this is my new home and you have the first letter. The afternoon gets darker and the wind is blowing around the house. Instead of the birds at my old home, there are seagulls fighting for fish and last-found kernels in the field.

It is All Saints Day. Every year I think back to Germany when, on this day, we go to the cemeteries to bring flowers and visit our loved ones who left this earth.

Also visit with people at the graveside to rekindle memories. The smell of fall flowers and the last fires of the burning potato vines and leaves hang over the harvested fields. In contrast to the old country, here we concentrate more on the Halloween fun and carved pumpkins. I visited Egg Harbor a couple of weeks ago. A small, growing village which has a traditional Pumpkin Patch Festival. Every storefront and house was decorated and I enjoyed taking many photos of the "pumpkin people." I got a great shot outside of Jane's Designs for Women, a unique woman's clothing boutique.

November--the month of remembrance and for long letters. I will like living here.

Someone is knocking on the door. So long . . .

inge

November 12, 1996

Greetings from Gills Rock,

This evening is like a present. Dusk is falling and the rising hunter's moon is a small boat swimming through the sky. The rain from this morning has stopped.

When I told you in my last letter "someone is knocking on the door . . . " it was the club president, who came to invite me to join the oldest book club of Door County, the Door County Literary Guild. She lives in Egg

Harbor and asked me to give a short program this month. I am happy to meet new people and have chosen *Travel from the Early Centuries to Today.*

Every morning this month I read some poems. Today I choose "Autumn Day" by Rainer Maria Rilkes. This poem is exactly how I feel. The tree trunks shine silvery in their wetness and the early November rain was beating against the windows, where the half dead flies were buzzing; trying to dance with the raindrops. Everything lies in a soft, misty light. My chimes ring in the wind. The firewood crackles and the shadows of the flames flicker over the logs. The coffee is brewing and from the kitchen comes the smell of baking. I light the candles on the table. Through this visit from the president of the Guild and the invitation I was reminded of another book club I once joined.

We had just moved to the town on the river and I felt so at home, that in the first week I decided to become an American Citizen. The course was taught by a local couple and a history teacher. One day I read about a book club meeting and the teacher was named as the hostess. Since it was written up in the newspaper, I thought it was a public meeting and I called her up and asked if I could come. I was informed that it was a "private club." It was not long after, when I was invited for a meeting. Over thirty years later, I still remember my first evening and the program about a boat sailing through a hurricane. The presentation was spellbinding. The dessert was delicious. But the best part was the companionship. It was all so new to me.

Weeks later two of the women came to our house and invited me to join the club. One part of me cried, "Yes, I would like to." The other side asked, "Can I do it?" My husband encouraged me: "Yes, you can! Talk about what you read. Tell them in the first program where you came from and show your slides. They will only ask you once. This is your chance!" And with a grin, he added: "You can impress your new friends, when you show the university where I studied, which is older than the date the Mayflower arrived at Plymouth Rock."

It was the first slide program I gave in the United States. I prepared 14 days for it. I wrote and rewrote; but when the evening came, I just told the group about each picture and forgot about the written speech. Instead I talked from the heart. That evening was the cornerstone of an everlasting friendship. There were years of encouragement during hard times and happy sharing of the good times.

It was a fun group and for a long time I was the youngest member--always learning. While some of the others told about their grandchildren, my daughter was just entering grade school. We came together twice a month; it was a good way to leave the childrens' growing pains behind. I was helped through by wise and comforting talks. We all cared about each other. By sharing our lives I found that these friendships strengthened my love for the river town and the land.

Just two years later I became so sick with hepatitis that my family had to cope without me. The kids were brought to the hospital yard so I could wave to them from my window. They were not allowed to visit. Thanksgiving and the hunting season came and went. Telephone was the only communication with the outside world. Christmas season brought the news that my mother had died. I was allowed to go home, but my orders were "no work and no baking." That year the "girls" from the R.C. Book Club shared their cookies; helped decorate the Christmas tree; and wrapped the presents at my bedside. One couple invited us for Christmas dinner. I was so weak, but most importantly could still be with my family and friends. The sadness in me was turned into joy because of the sharing and kindness.

R.C. Book Club meetings continued throughout the seasons. We had summer picnics and Christmas parties. There was always laughter. All of the memories are coming back today and I wonder if the same bonding will happen again. The women of years ago made a strange town into a warm home. The oldest member gave me a tile once with these words: "You can hang this with your collection. May it remind you of the times we visited the Christmas Tree Farm!" Now it is hanging in my new kitchen here in Door. It seems that special tile made me remember all the things I write you today.

Our group was together for years. Then people moved away. Some died or retirement brought them more travels and the club became smaller. From eighteen to three, I got them to continue and we recruited new, younger members. But, it was the club itself that gave me the motivation to keep it going.

Once I was asked to give a program on "Real Relationships Between Friends and Strangers." When I came from the old country I was not only a stranger, but also a foreigner. Yet, I was included as a "friend" right away. Here, we all have lots of "friends," but the word "acquaintance" has become old-fashioned. A friend to me is a part of the soul. My friendships in Germany continue after years of only short visits and long letters. For a long time I was a wanderer between two worlds.

Often I was asked: "Where do you like it better?" The answer was always the same, "I lived 34 years in Germany, give me equal time here!" A place where you spent your childhood, school years and youth probably counts double. But my final decision was made the year my husband died. That's when I had to say good-bye to my best friend forever and continue with my children and friends I had made over the years. The ones from the R.C. Book Club gave me special support. I spent three months in Germany, but could not wait to return and stay in Wisconsin. It was home.

My mother recognized the difference a long time ago. When I left after visiting with her, she said, "When you lived in Illinois, you always said, 'We must go *back*.' But now since you lived in Wisconsin you say, 'I have to go *home*.'" Even my grandmother, who never knew I came here predicted that America was the land for me, "Once she's there, she never will come back to live here!"

You see, my friend, this afternoon and evening brought more and more reminiscence. If you don't have good memories, a rainy afternoon could make you feel lonely. Not me. I have many years of good family times, good travels, and good friends to remember in front of the fire.

It is getting late, and I will tell you more about my program when it is revised.

Thanks again for listening. Good night.

inge

November 30, 1998

Hello again from Door,

The last day of the month. The night was cold. A beautiful moon was shining and lit the path up to the house. It was a perfect atmosphere as I hosted my first Guild meeting. I had made some hot cider, tea with rum, coffee and Linzertorte. It smells so good throughout the house.

And I didn't have to worry at all about this group. The daughter of the charter member who gave my introduction at the first meeting two years ago, has become a great friend. Most of the "girls" knew each other for a longer time, but they made me, the newcomer, feel so welcome. There are such different tastes: one told me she loves romance novels; another likes mysteries; some go for politics and a few of us relish travel adventures. Finally it was my turn.

I thought back to earlier years and told them when I gave my first report on my little town in the Black Forest and its surroundings and said I would like to review three travel guides from Europe to America and vice versa: *An 1858 Handbook for Emigrants and Travelers*; Fielding's 1950 *Travel Guide to Europe* and my most used travel survival kit, *The Lonely Planet* from the 90's. Also some short chapters from *A Travel Guide to Europe 1492*. I emphasized how important letters of travelers are. Through them we know the journeys of St. Paul; Mozart's trip to Prague; Albrecht Duerer to Venice; Goethe to Rome. What once took months to travel--the same distance--is now only 3 hours.

So much knowledge has been gained from "then" to "now." There was a long discussion afterwards. I'm happy, but tired today . . . More later.

I'm awake at night
The blackbirds of thought
Fall over me--
Like into a field of wheat
After the harvest !
They are picking
And crying
And fighting.
I can not defend myself
Against them.
Or--can I ?
Just by listening
To the distant sound
Of a chime
Moving in the wind?
It is soothing.
It feels like the healing
Of a mother's hand.
The night
Lost the power of despair
And sleep takes me into
New tomorrows.

This morning I woke up and just knew the first snow has fallen! It is even more quiet outside and a defused light spills over my room, inviting me to stay in bed five minutes longer, just to enjoy the coziness. I thought back to last night and the difference between all the old book club members and now the Door County Guild.

Once I had joined a club as a young wife with a family. Now I am gray-haired, a senior living alone. Once glad to be out of the house for a change from the house work; now happy to fill out an evening with good company.

It was nice to share all the news with you over this month. In a way, it is my former R.C. Book Club friends who gave me this opportunity to write this all down. Thanksgiving was shared with the children and grandchildren. Since I have moved, it seems I do more cooking again. Here is the recipe you asked for.

We have early snow and the first cross-country skiers pass by the cabin. Glad my letters wanted to make you visit me here. I'm looking forward to your visit in May, when everything will be white again--not with snow, but with cherry blossoms.

Auf Wiedersehen, inge

P.S. Enjoy the recipes from the Guild members. They put together a cookbook to celebrate the 100th anniversary in 1999, *100 Years of Great Food, Good Books and Good Conversations.* I think the title is too long, but my Linzertorte is in it ! I had all the members sign a copy for you.

AMANDA BREKKE

December - Living in Two Lands
by
Ann Kurz Chambers

My house in Fish Creek is my grounded reality, a place where I work on my art--watercolors and leather works that I sell at J. Jeffrey Taylor's Gallery. It's where I maintain close ties to old friends; do the ordinary things that lend stability and a sense of place to one's life.

It is a ranch-style home, set among birch and maple trees which partially shade a large patio. Inside the house, a field stone fireplace gives me warmth on cold December days. The flagstone floor is easy to keep clean, as is the simple floor plan: a kitchen and living area all-in-one with my studio area at one end of the room. Large floor to ceiling windows fill my need for sunlight and makes the outdoors part of my indoors. I'm happy to be settled here from November to May. In that way, I'm an unusual Door resident. Most people come during the peak season. But I leave when the hustle and bustle begins. The perfect time for me to head to my other spiritual home located on top of a mountain in Colorado.

I bought 35 acres in western Colorado eight years ago when my need for wide open space, a lifelong yearning to live in the West and a search for soulfulness became a psychic necessity after the divorce. My sons and I built a simple cabin that first autumn in Colorado. Sixteen by twenty feet with a loft for sleeping. Perhaps, because of my life since the divorce and the struggle to make a living as an artist, my cabin and the land did become a true sanctuary for me--a safe place--a safe house.

For two years after we built the cabin I could only stop at it when I did trips to art festivals on the West Coast. But in 1993, I decided to take a year off. A sabbatical. I rented out my Door County house and lived in the cabin with one of my sons for the winter of 1993-94. I felt a great need to simplify my life, to reflect, to just rest. I was burned-out from working so hard. My life and attitude had become so bitter and lacking any joy. I needed to just "be."

In her book, *We Took to the Woods*, Louise Dickinson Rich describes the adventures, hard work and pleasures of living a primitive life in the Maine woods in 1942. I came across the book on my mother's parlor library shelf when we sold her cottage and moved her to a nursing home. I read the book and could readily identify with Rich's struggles and everyday demands to just fulfill the essentials of daily life in an isolated area. Visitors to Rich's cabin would continually ask, "Why don't you write a book? Don't you get bored? What do you do all day? Aren't you ever frightened? Do you get out very often?" I felt a kindred soul in Louise and identified with her tribulations, satisfactions and at times, uncertainties. I found, as she did, that one can find peace by leading a life bound by everyday simple pleasures. No frills.

My journal entry from December 14, 1993 recounts some of the flavor of my daily life during that year when I took to the woods.

MONDAY. I am sitting at my work table, typing on my old portable typewriter with cold fingers. My work area is on the second floor of our two-story, twenty-foot by forty-foot barn. I look out a big window and see the cabin and drive-way, 300 feet down the hill. I started a fire in the small wood stove downstairs a few minutes ago. The heat will slowly come up through the opening to the second floor. I have gotten skilled at starting fires --I am now the "One Match Wonder." The thermometer inside reads 32 degrees. My sorrel boots, sweat pants, sweater, vest and hat keep me comfortable until I feed the stove enough times to get the upstairs temperature to 50 degrees, usually as high as I can get it. I found that I learned to adjust to cooler temperatures.

TUESDAY. I didn't build a fire in the cabin stove last night. This morning the temperature inside the cabin was 40 degrees and the outside temperature was 2 degrees--a sparkling, sunny day, quiet, with 18 inches of snow. Yesterday, while I was sitting here at my work table, I looked down to see a short-tailed weasel diving and cavorting in the snow as if it were water. He popped up and dove down under the white piles. When he came up a few minutes later, he had a mouse in his mouth and ran with it under the barn. He lives there and stockpiles dead mice in his "larder."

I bought a bright yellow Meyer's snowplow in Denver,

hauled it in my utility trailer to the cabin, November 4. The snow came that night--twelve inches. First snow of the season. My son Sam installed the plow on his F250, 1973 Ford truck, a monster with 36-inch knobby tires. I needed a plow to get in and out from my cabin to the main road, 10 miles away. Sam has lived here the previous winters and has managed to drive up most of the time because the neighbor--one-half mile from us--plowed most of the road. Then Sam would walk the one-half mile from our gate to the cabin. He and the neighbor hired a grader to dig out the road when it got so narrow that there was no where to push the snow. One year they had to have it done two times.

WEDNESDAY. I usually go to town every ten days. I have been lucky with the weather and I haven't had the problem of getting stuck or having to use the tire chains I keep in the van at all times. "Town" is Glenwood Springs which is located about twenty miles down a winding mountain road. Eight miles of it narrow with twelve inches of deep, impassable mud in the spring.

We have five buildings: the cabin, barn, outhouse, bath house and shed. The outhouse is 4 feet by 8 feet. I have tiled the floor and the toilet platform. I used my Columbine tiles on the walls. A standard toilet seat, wood plaques, with whimsical verses, photos and the usual wire toilet roll dispenser grace our "privy." It also has a sink (water in a jug and bucket for a drain), and a vanity that faces South with a dropdead gorgeous view of the mountains. An outhouse with a view? Why not. I am not concerned with privacy here. The gable ends on the roof are adorned with elk horns and antlers bleached white. Accented with cedar shakes, it is really quaint.

104

THURSDAY. We built an eight-foot shed in 1990, just before the first November snow. I was nailing the last of the shingles when the four day storm hit. The cabin was built in August, 1990. Pine-paneled and every inch of space used for best efficiency. My older son, Sim, and I picked out every board of paneling and loaded it onto the old pick-up truck. We almost lost a load just two miles from the cabin. We backed the truck up the road for the remainder of that lumber run. I installed my hand-painted Columbine tiles (Columbine is the state flower of Colorado) on my counter top, by the stove and on the floor by the door. We are still using the subfloor until we can plank it with pine. Growing up with a father who was an industrial arts instructor has definitely come in handy.

FRIDAY. We installed propane lamps this year which is an improvement over candles, kerosene lamps and propane lanterns which seem to rapidly lose their light. I also use one of my mother's old kerosene chimney lamps to read by. I have to use one when I work in the barn after dark. My propane gas kitchen range makes life easier when I cook. I keep a blue porcelain pot of water on the wood stove for washing dishes. A pitcher pump by the double stainless steel sink gives us water for washing and bathing. We probably wouldn't get sick if we drank from the tank, but we choose to get water more directly from the spring. The pitcher pump draws from a 450 gallon storage tank in the crawl space which I filled November 7 before the pipe froze. I have a spring 300 feet up the hill from the cabin, behind the barn. A black PVC pipe runs the water by gravity to a 75 gallon rubber tub outside the cabin, just off the West deck. The volume of water varies with the season. In spring and summer, about 10 gallons a minute; in the fall and late summer there's a steady drip. I listen for that sound. It is part of the cabin. Not to hear it, causes me great concern. To dig a well would cost between $2,000 and $10,000. It is a real gamble as good water could be at any depth. Sometimes the spring stops. I think the pipe gets a vapor lock in the heat of the day. Of course, in the winter, we have no running water from the spring. So, in winter, I hike to the spring, through knee-deep snow (or higher) and sit for an hour filling gallon milk jugs which I load onto a sled and drag down the hill to the cabin. I don't mind the simple task. I sit, look at the snow, rocks, birds and blue sky and enjoy the peace I feel here.

SATURDAY. Sam and I hauled two loads of firewood for the barn and put three cords of wood in the shed behind the cabin. He had cut and split mostly aspen and oak last year. We struggled through the snow two weeks ago to cut more dead aspen and haul it to our parking area for Sam to split. It was a good task and something to do on a beautiful, sun-filled day.

SUNDAY. The climate here takes an adjustment. The latitude and altitude affect the intensity of the sun. Sometimes I do not start a fire in the cabin in the morning because the sun can heat it up to over 80 degrees in the winter. Even on the coldest days, the sun makes a warming difference.

MONDAY. My son, Sim, and I built an eight foot square bath house last June. We built a redwood bench, a vanity with sink surrounded by my "steer head" tiles. We use the eight-foot dimension as plywood and siding are four-by-eight-foot sheets. The bath house has a big mirror, a glass door facing South, and large glass walls facing South and West. Again, as in the outhouse, my privacy is not a concern. The view and the warming of the sun are more important. On the roof a plastic dome gives more light and heat. I took a bath in there last Friday--hard to believe it could get that warm in December. I had covered the decking floor with black plastic to keep the wind from coming through the cracks. We use "solar showers," heavy plastic bags, black on one side and clear on the other. I heat the water by laying the bags clear side up and letting the sun do its job. This works only in spring through early fall, as the cold air cools the water too fast. For this bath, I warmed the water on the floor of the cabin: hung the bag from the harness hook in the bath house and felt exhilarated. Otherwise sponge baths in a large bowl have to do.

TUESDAY. Most nights in bed by 9:00 p.m. I bought a cellular phone for emergencies and to call my other children. Sometimes the signal is not very strong. To charge the phone (we have no electricity) I always plug it in the cigarette lighter on every trip to town.

WEDNESDAY. It is quiet here. I am getting my psychic rest by doing basic life sustaining tasks: filling the wood box, getting water, making bread, cooking, keeping fires going in two buildings, shoveling snow, and keeping food outside in an eight foot long wood bin that freezes most things but protects it in all seasons from the bobcats, porcupines, skunks and bears.

THURSDAY.   Our milk usually has ice crystals in it. Getting used to having to plan ahead to thaw leftovers and orange juice.   I have one small ice chest that I take in and out at night to keep vegetables from freezing--not always successfully.   I am isolated, but I really don't mind.   I usually take a walk to the lower gate (one and one-half miles) every day in late afternoon.   It is quite a work out as, on the way home, it is an uphill climb.   I stop less and less to catch my breath.   The altitude (cabin is at about 8300 feet) and the cold causes the lungs to gasp for air.   However, with normal activities one doesn't notice any difference.   I haven't had my cross country skiis out yet.   I will learn to use snowshoes as they are more effective for walking in the woods.   The elk were here ten days ago, on the driveway.

FRIDAY.   In the first month I was here we skinned and cut up and deboned all the meat from three deer, one cow elk and one calf elk.   The two elk took three of us six hours working steadily on the table in the cabin.   Sam and his friend shot the animals on the adjacent lot.   We keep some meat here, but Sam's friend has freezers.   I made jerky out of 25 pounds of meat.   It was tricky to get the smokey fire going and to keep it going.   I used the barrel smoker that my Dad used for smoking carp in Wisconsin.   Some of the jerky got a really strong taste from the smoke.

SATURDAY.   When it snows I sweep or shovel the 900 square feet of redwood deck and let the sun melt the rest and dry it off.   I go to town to do our laundry--$1.50 a load.   I dry the clothes partially and then bring them home to hang in the bath house or on hooks and chairs in the cabin. We wear our clothes until they really need to be washed. When I go to town I buy a <u>Wall Street Journal</u> and a <u>USA Today</u> which I savor and parcel out for the next few days. A friend lent me a box of those silly romantic novels. I quit work for the day at about 4:00 p.m. For a while I read one or two books daily.

SUNDAY. I can see South from the front of the cabin 40 miles to Mt. Sopris, Capital Peak and Chair Mountain. I can see the Snow Cats at night, working on the ski runs on Snowmass Mountain. The changes in light, weather and clouds give me great pleasure. My entire scope of vision is 180 degrees from East to West. I can finally SEE!

The coyotes often howl and yip, thrilling me with their wild song. Nights with a full moon are so bright I don't need a flashlight outside. I'd swear the stars are closer here. I need to get a book on the constellations and learn more about this new part of my world.

MONDAY. In "the Door," in Fish Creek. I'm more relaxed and rested. Not sure of the future, but not obsessing over it anymore. I'm really trying to live in the moment like Frances Hamerstrom always recommended.

Balance was restored during that winter of seclusion. Louise Rich believes that discontent is the fear of missing something and contentment is the knowledge that you aren't missing anything. I am content and happy to have two places to live that I enjoy immensely. Life does constantly change. For me, having my Colorado land as a sanctuary grounds me enough to endure and embrace those changes. As I sit by the fire, here in my Fish Creek "nest," I am enjoying a cup of cranberry tea. Waiting for my Guild friends to join me. December is a time to settle in, to be cozy, to have long nights to ponder and marvel at the mysteries of life.

The cranberry bread will be ready shortly. I'll brew some more tea and prepare some hazelnut coffee. I know Kate will like that. Tonight rounds out another year for the "girls."

KATE & MELANIE

Last Half of the January Interview
by
Mary "Casey" Martin

Kate thought, *Well, I haven't bored her to tears, but I better wrap this interview up or the "girls" will show up and I won't have the Caribbean Cream Sauce ready. The pork tenderloin had browned evenly in the oven.* Kate felt the need to tell Melanie her story, too. "So, that's the women of Door County's oldest club. And tonight's meeting with the Guild members is more than just our 100th anniversary kick-off. It's my farewell bash. I have to leave my beloved Door, at least for a while."

Melanie looked puzzled. After all she had heard about the twelve women, she knew how integral Kate was in the diverse role as leader, but more so, as friend to the members of this unique Literary Guild. She questioned Kate, "Why would you leave now?"

"An employment opportunity came up that I would be foolish to pass up, especially at my age. Writing has taken me away from Door and brought me back again. Not everyone gets the chance to come home again. And I did. Who knows? Maybe I will return in the future if the gods smile down on me once more." Kate explained. Then added, "Do you need anything else?"

Melanie was packing her equipment up. She closed her notebook and was putting on her coat when she remembered, "Yes, the cookbook. You promised me a copy of the 100th Anniversary cookbook. I can use it as part of the story. The proceeds of any sales go to the Door County Literacy Council, right? $15.95 each and they mail the checks to Beverly Thiel, P.O. Box 15, Jacksonport, WI ?"

"You've got it all," Kate acknowledged as she handed her a copy of the cookbook. "Let me help you to the door. And thanks again for coming out in this awful weather. I hope it has stopped snowing for good. We all appreciate the coverage for the Guild and the Literacy Council."

Melanie turned after opening the door, "I want to wish you a safe journey, too, Kate . . . as you go off on your new employment adventure. It was great to meet you." Then she sincerely added, "Stay tuned."

Kate couldn't tell her the whole story. Her life for the last two years had become too complicated. Born and raised on the peninsula, she needed to see more of the world. Her journalism degree from the University of Wisconsin-Madison did that for her. After 30 years of traveling, she had to come back to see if she could live in Door full time. Back for five years, now she longed for a change of scenery. The relationship Kate got involved in over the last two years seemed like a very natural progression of a friendship. She, a writer, working on stories for the Door County Chamber of Commerce and other businesses had put her in close contact, too close, to some of the most charming people on the peninsula. One business man in particular who was the subject of numerous personal interviews.

Ten years younger than Kate, he was tall, dark and handsome. His full, black mustache tickled more than her nose. His gray blue chamelion eyes were the second distinguishing characteristic she found irresistible, but it was really his quick wit and humor that attracted her to him. No one had made her laugh that hard, or that long for many years. Innocent teasing had turned into heated passion on more than one occasion. He was married, of course. Very married.

It wasn't that there was really any false hope of him leaving his wife. That wasn't it. It was well understood by Kate that he would never leave. "12 years," his wife would say at every opportunity. Anytime anyone was in earshot, she would announce to the world their lasting bond and flash her band of gold.

His commitment to the family was admirable. No, certainly none of that would be the reason for Kate's leaving. If anything, those things again drew her toward him--broadened her respect for him. A good man who was dedicated to his family and his business.

What Kate absolutely couldn't deal with right now was--the change. And how could he deal with it? How many years had it been? He and his wife had moved to Door from Dubuque. They had three children. So this was the farthest thing from Kate's mind.

Kate would have never known if it hadn't been for the research on this final article. His wife's name just wasn't checking out for the backstory. Her close call with cancer didn't make any alarms go off, until the doctor slipped. Her woman's intuition kicked in. *Always trust your gut.*

The reporter in her couldn't let the question go un-answered and she couldn't confront him with the bizarre idea until it was checked out. Now it did check out. Kate was having a lot of problems dealing with the fact that the man she loved, was married--in reality to another MAN! Man? Sex change in 1984? Children adopted? It was more than she could handle right now.

A trip to Italy was on her mind for a long time. She could visit Frederico, an old friend who lived near Venice. This was the perfect opportunity to go . . . NOW. And enough miles and an ocean to separate her from the pain. Then, by the end of May, Amanda would be at her cozy cabin in Colorado and Kate could find safe refuge there for a few months. Louise could keep an eye on her house until she decides what she wants to do. The Guild would go on . . . Beverly was the incoming president; new members were being sought and the TV interview was done.

Almost everyone accepted the "employment op-portunity" scenario--no problems there. The worst part of the whole thing has been keeping the secret from Louise. It wouldn't serve any purpose for anyone else besides Amanda to know at this point, would it? The only life really changed she believed, is her own.

Saved again by her Door chimes . . . Louise shouts hello and bursts in with a beautiful cake: *Happy 100th Anniversary & Bon Voyage* are inscribed on the top.

The perfect hostess, Kate enters from the kitchen, "Welcome friend. Make yourself at home . . . I have to finish the cream sauce . . . " All the time, in the back of her mind, she's thinking, *What will next year bring?*

Twelve recipes from the D C Literary Guild's cookbook appear after What's Next?.

WHAT'S NEXT?

Here's what happens to everyone
as the New Year begins:

MELANIE RICHARDS, the Green Bay television reporter, had moved to Door County six months earlier from San Francisco where she was working for NBC and volunteering at an AIDS clinic. One of her recent assignments was interviewing Kate Murphy.

KATHERINE "KATE" MURPHY left on Valentine's Day for Italy and eventually would meet up with Amanda at her Colorado retreat. She was excited by the possibilities of her new job.

HANNAH VILAS planned a new travel adventure and published a cookbook of her favorite dishes.

BEVERLY THIEL became an artist. An art critic vacationing on "the Door" ran across her oil paintings of the spring ice-jambs and described them as "rather Georgia O'Keeffe-like, strangely lurid."

ANNA PEDERSON finds solace in her child's 11 godmothers. She and the baby are doing fine. The father of Anna's child watches from his tractor in sorrow that he has not the courage to claim his son.

SALLY APPLEBACH began reading poetry to Thad and they moved back to Door County.

EDIE SUMMERS changed her name to Walking Sage and teaches writing courses on a North Dakota Indian reservation.

LOUISE SORENSON found out on Christmas Eve that her daughter became engaged. The wedding date is set--July 4, 1999.

GAIL ANDERSON booked another EarthView trip to study Siberian cranes in Lan Zhou, China.

JERRALYN SAUNDERS grieved her father's death, but found happiness with a new love interest she met at the funeral home.

EMMI JOHNSTON was invited to exhibit her collection, "Works by Water and Wind" at an avant garde gallery in Minneapolis, MN.

INGE MUELLER won a prestigious photography award and was commissioned to do a book about traveling around the world in 60 days.

AMANDA BREKKE found someone to share her Colorado home and life. She sold her Door County property to the highest bidder.

THE DOOR COUNTY LITERARY GUILD COOKBOOK went into a second printing before the end of 1999.

THE GUILD'S COOKBOOK

JANUARY
Kate's Pork Tenderloin   Mary "Casey" Martin
with Caribbean Cream Sauce
using Lehmann Farms Haute Caribbean Seasoning

FEBRUARY
Hannah's Matzos Cake   Edith Nash

MARCH
Beverly's Potato Soup   Justin Isherwood

APRIL
Anna's Pound Cake   Barbara Fitz Vroman

MAY
Sally's Banana Cream Pie   Mariann Ritzer

JUNE
Edie's Creamed Vegetables with Coconut   Jackie Langetieg

JULY
Louise's Fish Boil Courtesy of Jeanne Larson Hyde
from her cookbook, *Hazel's Kitchen Table*

AUGUST
Gail's Peanut Butter & Squash Soup Mary "Casey" Martin

SEPTEMBER
Jerralyn's Gourmet Pizza on the Grill Steve Raap

OCTOBER
Emmi's Apple Pretty DyAnne Korda
from *Wise Woman's Garden*

NOVEMBER
Inge's Linzertorte Ilse Dietsche

DECEMBER
Amanda's Classic Cranberry Bread Ann Kurz Chambers

KATE'S PORK TENDERLOIN with CARIBBEAN CREAM SAUCE

1 TBLS.		Olive Oil
1		Pork Tenderloin
1		Green Pepper, seeded and sliced
2		Carrots, cut up
2		Celery Stalks, cut up
1		Onion, medium, sliced
4-6		Fresh Mushrooms, sliced
1	tsp.	Salt
1/2	tsp.	Fresh Ground Pepper
1	clove	Garlic, peeled and sliced
1	TBLS.	Beef Broth in 1 cup water
1-2	tsp.	*Lehmann Farms Haute Caribbean Seasoning*
1	TBLS.	Fresh Lemon Juice
1	can	Mushroom Soup, 10 oz.
or 1	cup	Cream

Shake 1 tsp. of *Lehmann Farms Haute Caribbean Seasoning* on top of Pork Tenderloin.

Brown the Pork Tenderloin in a pan seasoned with salt, pepper, onions and garlic and olive oil. Reduce heat to medium.

Add green pepper, carrots, celery and fresh mushrooms to the pan. Squeeze fresh lemon juice (and shake additional *Haute Caribbean Seasoning* if desired) over vegetables.

Add beef broth in water. Saute another 15 minutes.

Add can of Mushroom Soup and continue cooking until pork tenderloin is cooked through. Approximately another 15 to 20 minutes.

Slice tenderloin into medallions and serve. Serves 4.

OPTIONAL: Add a dollop of sour cream and sliced tomatoes.

HANNAH'S MATZOS CAKE

| 1 dozen | Large Eggs, room temp., separated |
| 2 cups | Granulated Sugar |

1 cup	Matzo <u>Cake</u> Flour or Meal, sifted
and 1 cup	Potato Flour, sifted
or 2/3 cup	Potato Starch, sifted

<u>Prepare fruit ahead:</u>

1	Orange, zest and juice
1	Lemon, zest and juice
1	Apple, peeled and cored, grated fine
1	Banana, mashed

Preheat oven to 350 degrees.
Grease and flour BOTTOM ONLY of angel cake pan.
10 X 4 1/2" holds 20 cups. DO NOT GREASE SIDES !

Beat whites until stiff, put aside.
Beat yolks and sugar until it makes the ribbon.
Add fruits, beat well. Add sifted flours.
When thoroughly mixed, add stiff whites, fold with hand.
Pour batter into pan and place on upper third rack for
55 minutes, then test. Cover with foil if it needs another
10 minutes.

BEVERLY'S POTATO SOUP

Set a dozen medium-sized potatoes on a back porch over night in mid winter. Cover with an old dog blanket. Retrieve the now chilled potatoes (about 35 degrees Fahrenheit) late in the afternoon the following day.

Peel sparingly if early winter. Peel more completely if late winter. Rinse, cut intoquarter sections or smaller.

With a clean stone-dressers hammer (the kind used to shape tombstones), press against the potato with sufficient force to crush, place remains in pot with water to cover.

Boil until pieces are tender; mash again with standard kitchen utensil.

Saute ingredients together in butter for five minutes:

Okra, according to taste, about one quart.

2 cups celery, chopped

1 green pepper, seeded and diced small

2 medium onions, the method of dismemberment left to your personal choice.

Add all vegetables together with smushed potatoes in a commodious pot, adding enough water only to cook thoroughly.

Stir. Simmer.

Salt to taste. Black pepper, too.

Simmer some more, until a semi-tractable quaking bog sort of consistancy is acquired.

Remove from heat.

Set table deliberately. A red checked cloth is best. The candles ought be long tapers set into driftwood.

Large soup bowls, prewarmed.

The champagne to be served in long stem flutes.

Stoke the fireplace well.

Dress provocatively.

Serve. Simmer. Stir. Simmer.

ANNA'S POUND CAKE
with Door County Cherries

1/2 pound	Butter or Margarine
2 cups	Granulated Sugar
1 tsp.	Vanilla Extract
5	Large Eggs (add one at a time)
2 cups	All Purpose Flour

Preheat oven to 350 degrees.

Grease and flour 10 inch tube pan.

Beat butter till light and fluffy; add other ingredients gradually in order listed. Beat well after each addition. It's important to beat well for the cake to be light and airy.

Pour batter into pan.

Bake for about one hour. Test with a toothpick. Let cool for 5 minutes before removing from pan.

Serve with slightly sweetened whipped cream and fresh Door County cherries or whatever embellishment your heart desires.

SALLY'S BANANA CREAM PIE

In top of double boiler, mix well:

3/4 cup	Sugar
7 TBLS.	Flour
1/4 tsp.	Salt

Next, in seperate bowl, beat:

3	Large Eggs Yolks
2 cups	Milk
1/2 tsp.	Vanilla

Gradually add liquid to flour mix, stirring until smooth.

Cook the above ingredients in double boiler over hot water about 20 minutes or until filling is thickened.
Then cool.

MERINGUE:

1/2 cup	Sugar
3	Egg Whites, measure in cup
1/4 tsp.	Tartar

Best results when adding as much sugar as egg whites.
Measure egg whites in cup and beat till foamy.
Gradually add equal amount of sugar till very stiff
    peaks form.
Put meringue on pie. Make sure it touches all edges
    of the pie or it will shrink in the middle.

Preheat oven to 350 degrees.
Slice bananas in pie crust. Alternate filling with more bananas. Top with meringue.
Bake 8 to 10 minutes until the meringue browns.

EDIE'S CREAMED VEGETABLES with COCONUT

2		Tomatoes, medium-sized, seeded and skinned
2	cups	Unsweetened Coconut, grated
2	cups	Milk
2		Garlic Cloves, medium-sized, minced
1 - 2	TBLS.	Ginger, fresh, minced
2	cups	Onions, chopped (Option: add celery)
1	TBLS.	Peanut Oil
1 1/2	tsp.	Turmeric
1	tsp.	Lemon Grass, fresh or dried, crumbled
1	tsp.	Chili Powder
1/2	lb.	Tofu, firm, diced
		Crushed Red Pepper, to taste
1/2	lb.	Green Beans, fresh, cut in 1 1/2-in lengths.
1/4 -1/2	cup	Water, as needed.
3 - 4	cups	Broccoli, chopped

Heat saucepan of water to boiling. Core tomatoes and drop into the water for a slow count of 10. Remove and peel under cold running water. Cut the tomatoes open and squeeze out and discard seeds. Chop the tomatoes into cubes and set aside.

Lightly toast 1/2 the coconut and set aside. Place the rest in a saucepan with milk. Heat to boiling point. Remove from heat and allow to cool to room temerature. Puree in a blender, then strain, reserving the milk. Discard the coconut. after pressing out all liquid.

In a deep skillet, saute garlic, ginger, and onion in oil with salt. Add turmeric, lemon grass, chili powder, tofu and red pepper. Saute over medium heat for five minutes.

Stir in beans and 1/4 water. Cover and cook for 5to 8 minutes, stirring occasionally. Add more water if necessary.

Add broccoli, tomatoes, and coconut milk. Mix well and cover. Continue cooking until broccoli is bright green.

Serve with wild or yellow rice. Top with toasted coconut.

LOUISE'S FISH BOIL
from Jeanne Larson Hyde's cookbook,
Hazel's Kitchen Table

4 pounds	Red Potatoes, small
16	White Onions, small
10 quarts	Water
1 cup	Salt, divided
8 pounds	Trout, cut up into 2-inch chunks (Whitefish may be substituted)

Wash potatoes and cut a small slice off each end.
Place in a bowl of cold water until ready to use.
Peel onions.
Heat water in a large, deep kettle with strainer until
boiling. Add potatoes, onions and 1/2 cup of the salt.
When water returns to a rolling boil, boil 12 minutes.
Add fish and remaining 1/2 cup salt.
Return to rolling boil again. Boil 11 minutes.
(Do NOT overcook or fish will fall apart.) Lift strainer
from water and drain. Rinse fish lightly. Serve with
coleslaw, rye bread and cherry pie.

COLESLAW

8 cups	Cabbage, shredded
2/3 cup	Salad Dressing
2 tsp.	Sugar
1 tsp.	Lemon Juice
1 tsp.	Celery Salt

Place cabbage in a large bowl. In a small bowl, stir
together salad dressing, sugar, lemon juice and celery salt.
Pour over cabbage; blend well.

GAIL'S PEANUT BUTTER & SQUASH SOUP

1	Butternut Squash, medium (2 lbs.), unpeeled
4 cups	Chicken Broth
1	Apple, large, tart, peeled, cored, cut in eighths
1	Onion, quartered
1/2 cup	Peanut Butter, smooth
1 tsp.	Curry Powder
1/2 tsp.	Salt
	Pepper to taste
1/2 cup	Cream

In large heavy pot bring broth to a boil.

Cut squash in 2-inch pieces; discard seed and stringy portions.

Add squash, apple and onion. Reduce heat; cover and simmer for 20 minutes or until squash, apple and onion are very tender.

Stir in peanut butter, curry powder, salt and pepper until well-blended.

In blender or food processor, puree' 2 cups soup at a time until smooth. Return to pot; stir in cream.

Heat through. Serve immediately in warmed soup bowls.

OPTIONAL TOPPINGS: Shake a little paprika on top and add a sprig of parsley.

JERRALYN'S GOURMET PIZZA ON THE GRILL

1 tsp.	Olive Oil
1	Frozen Pizza Dough, thawed
2	Tomatoes, fresh, sliced thin
1	Yellow Pepper, seeded and sliced
1	Green Pepper, seeded and sliced
1 lb.	Mushrooms, sliced thick
1 can	Artichoke Hearts, chopped
1 lb.	Monterey Jack Cheese, shaved
1/2 lb.	Medium Sharp Cheddar, shaved
1/2 lb.	Pepper Cheese, shaved

Prepare grill. Tin foil may be used as cooking surface on rack of grill.

Apply Olive Oil onto to rack or foil.

Prepare pizza dough and also drizzle olive oil onto top of pizza dough. Add fresh vegetables and cover. Cook for 10 minutes until vegetables are tender.

Add cheeses until all melt and serve.

OPTIONAL TOPPINGS: Shrimp, scallops, whitefish, swordfish or tuna.

EMMI'S APPLE PRETTY
from *Wise Woman's Garden*

1 cup	Brown Sugar
1/2 cup	Butter or Margarine
1	Egg (or 2 Egg Whites)
1 1/2 cup	Flour
1/2 tsp.	Cinnamon
1/4 tsp.	Cloves, ground
1/4 tsp.	Nutmeg, fresh, grated
1 tsp.	Baking Soda
1/2 cup	Coffee, cold and stiff
1/2 cup	Currants
1 cup	Apple, cored, pared and chopped pretty
1/2 cup	Nuts, of your choice . . . Try Hickory.

Heat oven to 375 degrees.

Combine coffee, fruit and nuts. Let seethe as silent as a crypt.

Cream sugar and butter.

Add egg.

Sift flour, spices and baking soda.

Stir dry ingredients alternately with wet and chunky things into sugar-butter-egg batter.

Put to bed in a loaf pan.

Bake for 45 minutes.

INGE'S LINZERTORTE

3	Butter Sticks
2 1/2 cups	Flour
1 1/3 cups	Sugar
2 cups	Hazelnuts, ground (or Almonds)
1	Egg
3 tsp.	Cocoa
1 tsp.	Cinnamon
1/4 tsp.	Cloves, ground
2 tsp.	Raspberry Schnapps
	(or German Kirschwasser)
1 8 oz.	Raspberry Marmalade
1	Egg yolk mixed with a litttle water.

Preheat oven to 375 degrees.

Cut butter into flour. Fold in other ingredients.

Let dough rest for one hour. Roll out the dough and press about 3/4 of it into a long baking sheet. (Save 1/4)

Spread on marmalade. Cut the rest of the dough in small strips and lay in a lattice pattern over the filling.

Brush with egg yolk and water.

Bake for about one hour. Let cool and cut at an angle for individual pieces.

AMANDA'S CLASSIC CRANBERRY BREAD

2 cups	Flour, all purpose
1 cup	Sugar
1 1/2 tsp.	Baking Powder
1 tsp.	Salt
1/2 tsp.	Baking Soda
2 TBLS.	Shortening
1 TBLS.	Orange Peel, grated
3/4 cup	Orange Juice
1	Egg, well-beaten
1 - 2 cups	Cranberries, fresh or frozen, chopped
1/2 cups	Nuts, chopped

Preheat oven to 350 degrees.

Grease BOTTOM ONLY of a 9 X 5 loaf pan.

In a bowl, mix together flour, sugar, baking powder, salt and baking soda.

Stir orange juice, orange peel, shortening and egg into dry ingredients. Mix until well-blended.

Stir in cranberries and chopped nuts.

Pour batter into loaf pan.

Bake for 55 to 60 minutes or until toothpick inserted in center of loaf comes out clean. Cool thoroughly before serving.

THE GUILD'S READING LIST

JANUARY
And Ladies of the Club   Helen Hooven Santmyer
Hazel's Kitchen Table   Jeanne Larson Hyde
Cooking in Door County   Pauline Wanderer

FEBRUARY
Margaret Mead: A Life   Jane Howard
With A Daughter's Eye   Cathy Bateson

MARCH
A Rose for Emily   William Faulkner

APRIL
Door Way   Norbert Blei
Fish Creek Voices   Ed & Lois Schreiber

MAY
Simple Passion   Annie Ernaux
What We Carry   Dorianne Laux

JUNE
A Match to the Heart   Gretel Ehrlich
The Dinner Party   Judy Chicago

JULY
Bridges of Madison County   Robert James Waller

AUGUST
The Snows of Kilimanjaro   Ernest Hemmingway

SEPTEMBER
Half Asleep in Frog Pajamas   Tom Robbins

OCTOBER

Montana 1948	Larry Watson
Justice	Larry Watson
One Hundred Years of Solitude	Gabriel Garcia Marquez
Griffin and Sabine	Nick Bantock
Sabine's Notebook	Nick Bantock
The Golden Mean	Nick Bantock
Dreaming in Cuban	Cristina Garcia

NOVEMBER

Travel from the Early Centuries to Today
An 1858 Handbook for Emigrants and Travelers
Feilding's 1950 Travel Guide to Europe
The Lonely Planet
A Travel Guide to Europe 1942

DECEMBER

We Took to the Woods	Louise Dickinson Rich

Other Poets, Writers and Artists Mentioned:

Gregory Bateson
Chekhov
Julia Child
Countee Cullen
Ram Dass
Charles Dickens
Emily Dickinson
Clyde Edgerton
T.S. Eliot
Sigmund Freud
Betty Friedan
Germaine Greer

Joy Harjo
Langston Hughes
Victor Hugo
John Irving
Rabbi Harold Kushner
Margaret Mead
M. Scott Peck
Rainer Maria Rilkes
Margaret Sanger
Sappho
Gloria Steinem
Sojourner Truth

P.D. Wodehouse
Virginia Woolf